THE BURNING BABY
AND OTHER GHOSTS

A Geordie by birth, John Gordon moved to
East Anglia with his family during the Great
Depression, at the age of twelve. He served in
the Navy during the Second World War, and
afterwards worked on various local news-
papers. He is widely recognized as one of the
finest contemporary writers for young people.

Particularly well-known for his ghost stories,
he is the author of *The Ghost on the Hill*, *The
Giant Under the Snow*, *The House on the
Brink* and *The Grasshopper*, as well as the
Teenage Memoir *Ordinary Seaman*. The Fens
landscape is an important presence in much
of his work, including *The Burning Baby*.
Married with two grown-up children, he now
lives in Norwich.

Other books by John Gordon

THE
BURNING
BABY

and other ghosts

JOHN GORDON

WALKER BOOKS
LONDON

For Robert

First published 1992 by Walker Books Ltd
87 Vauxhall Walk, London SE11 5HJ

This edition published 1993

© 1992 John Gordon

Printed and bound in Great Britain by
Cox and Wyman Ltd, Reading, Berkshire

British Library Cataloguing in Publication Data
A catalogue record for this book is
available from the British Library.

ISBN 0-7445-3080-6

CONTENTS

THE BURNING BABY

The morning after Barbara Pargeter disappeared, Bernard Friend rang the police.

"My God," he said, "I've just seen her parents and they're in a terrible state."

"Do you know the girl, sir?"

"Yes, I most certainly did. She was a nice kid."

"Still is, sir, we hope."

"Good grief!" He sucked in his breath. "What a terrible mistake."

"Quite understandable, sir."

"Excuse me." Bernard Friend wiped grease from his hands on to his overalls. He was sweating.

"Are you still there, sir?"

"I'm sorry, officer, but I was just thinking how I could have said the same thing to her parents ... the same slip of the tongue. I can't imagine what it might have done to her poor mum and dad." There was silence at the other end of the line, and he wiped his hands again. "They are very emotional about it," he said. "Very emotional."

"Yes, sir."

"Because Barbara Pargeter *is* a lovely little kid."

"She's nearly sixteen, sir."

"I know, I know – but time passes so quickly. It seems as if it was only yesterday when ... but I mustn't say everything that's in my heart at this moment in time. And I know – I mean I've been told – that girls of her age are a problem, aren't they? Not that I've had any experience of it. Not like you – someone in that line of business, girl business, as you might say."

Bernard Friend chuckled, but when there was still no response he added, "I suppose you have to deal with flighty little bits all the time, isn't that so? That way you must get to know what they are like, girls of that age. Always in trouble, I shouldn't wonder."

"Often enough, sir."

"And was she?"

"A flighty bit? Not that I'm aware of, Mr Friend."

"I mean was she in any trouble you know of?"

Papers were turned over. "May I ask exactly where you live, Mr Friend?"

"I'm just down the lane from the Pargeters. I have the garage. Friend's Motors."

"Ah," said the policeman, "now I've got you. The old car dump."

"Garage." His tone was pained. "I spend time and energy working for our little community and then a couple of them object to my business and it's instantly branded. Old motors are only part of my enterprise."

"Just trying to get you in my sights, Mr Friend."

"I'm having it landscaped because I am a caring sort of person. Which is why I am ringing you at this present moment in time when everybody is distressed about Miss Pargeter."

"Did I understand you to say that she had some sort of problem, Mr Friend?"

"No. Not as far as I know."

"I'm led to believe Barbara was an attractive young lady."

The sudden use of her first name made Bernard Friend clench his jaw. She had been missing for only one night but already the police were referring to her as *Barbara* as if her photograph had been on television, and journalists had been writing headlines.

"Attractive?" he said. "I don't know. Well … yes, maybe to a certain sort of individual."

"I see." The voice was flat, as if the policeman was taking notes. "Can you tell me when you last saw Barbara, Mr Friend?"

Bernard grunted to indicate that he had to think. "Hold on a sec." He gazed at the calendar on his office wall, working it out, and he used the pause to brush a fingertip under each eye to clear the beadlets of sweat. "It was the day before yesterday, I believe. Yes, that was it – I was on the pumps when she went by. On her way home, I presume."

"And how did she seem? Did she say anything?"

"Nothing, really. Just 'Hello, Mr Friend' – something like that. That was about teatime. I didn't see her after that. She was normal, absolutely normal, poor kid."

The officer, writing, repeated Bernard's words – "…and she said, 'Hello, Mr Friend'."

"If you are taking a statement, I'm very willing to help in any way possible – join a search party," said Bernard. "Anything."

"We hope that won't be necessary, Mr Friend. She's only been missing for one night, and our other enquiries may turn something up."

13

With the phone back on the hook, Bernard Friend gazed for a long time at the calendar before he realized he was looking at the picture of a girl; a naked girl with very long legs.

He was reaching to take it down when he paused. What garage didn't have such a calendar? People must have noticed it there, and to remove it would only make them think. Barbara herself had seen it.

He felt sweat on his back, but only for a moment – a cold dampness, soon gone. Barbara didn't matter any more. The damned calendar could stay where it was. It wasn't the calendar that was the problem; it was the breakdown truck. Once again the quick sweat came, but was soon mastered. The truck was far away; out of reach of any search parties around the village. Bernard Friend went back to work.

He was in the inspection pit, draining the sump of a Passat, when he saw a girl's feet as she walked across the floor towards him.

"Hello," he called.

There was no answer.

"Who's there?" He saw her shoes and ankles. They seemed familiar. "Who is it?"

There was a snuffle as if the girl was holding back her tears.

"Oh, hell!" He had tilted the can he was holding and black oil spilled down the front of his overalls. He cursed again and climbed out.

"So it's you," he said to the girl. "Look what you made me do." He picked a handful of waste from the bench and rubbed at the oil. "These overalls are

14

clean on today," he said. Then he realized, sickeningly, that he must not admit to having changed his clothes since yesterday. "Well, nearly clean. I've only had them on a week." He looked down. The knees and arms were already dirty, thank God. "Only a week," he said, "and look at them."

The girl obediently regarded his oily front, and nodded. The edges of her nose were red and her eyes were moist. "You're a mess," she said, and then put her knuckles to her mouth and added, "but where can Barbara have got to?" She wore a dark blue anorak and a grey school skirt. Her fair hair straggled down her cheeks and its untidiness made her appear younger than she was. "I'm scared, Bernie," she said.

"There's nothing to be scared of." He had a broad, handsome face and a dark moustache. It was a face taken from a movie poster, but the wide-shouldered, muscular body beneath it was not tall. He was barely the height of the girl who stood in front of him.

"Why are you scared, Julie?" he said. "She's only gone to a party, I expect, and spent the night with some feller." His deep laugh rumbled in his chest. "Some young chap's to blame."

Julie pulled her hands inside her sleeves. "Don't you mind?" she said.

"Me?" He raised one dark eyebrow. "Why should I mind? I'm old enough to be her father."

"I know, but..."

"But what, Julie?"

Faced with the intensity of his gaze, her eyes fell. "She used to talk to you, Bernie."

"Only out there by the pumps, Julie. You know that. Only by the pumps where everybody saw us."

"She was in trouble, Bernie." The words came out in a wail, and Julie's brimming eyes gazed tragically into his. "Trouble ... you know what I mean."

"I'm afraid I don't, Julie." His mouth had gone dry and his lips wanted to stick together.

"She said you knew all about it, Bernie."

"Me? Why me?" The pitch of his voice rose suddenly and alarmed him. "Excuse me, Julie, I've got a frog." He cleared his throat. "That's better." He frowned, thinking earnestly. "All she ever told me, Julie, was that she wasn't doing too well at school."

"That wasn't it, Bernie. She wasn't bothered about that."

He looked at her. This skinny girl was so bedraggled he thought it must be raining, and he could not prevent his eyes turning to the open door. Outside there was cold November sunlight but no rain. It was her misery that made her look like this, and girls in her state were dangerous. "Just what did she tell you, Julie?" he asked softly.

"She was in *trouble*." It was a whine of annoyance at his lack of understanding. "She was going to have a baby!"

"I don't believe it!" There were flecks of white at the corners of Bernard Friend's mouth. "I just don't believe it."

"It's true. She was pleased about it."

"Pleased?" But he knew very well what Barbara Pargeter had thought about having a baby, and a spurt of anger kept his voice strong and level. "Did she tell you who the father was?"

Julie shook her head.

"Nothing about him? Nothing at all?"

Julie shook her head again. "She just said she was pleased."

"Then what are you bothered about, Julie?" His voice rumbled with a relief he had to disguise. "I mean you *should* be bothered – *I'm* bothered about what you've just this minute told me – but if she was *happy*, it doesn't seem so bad."

"If she was happy why has she run away? It doesn't make sense, Bernie."

Two days ago he had enjoyed being called Bernie by kids, had encouraged it even, but now, on this girl's lips, it was too familiar, incriminating. "I don't know why you're telling me all this, Julie," he said. "I don't know you well enough, do I? All I ever did was chat to you two girls as you went by – when I wasn't busy." He picked up a wrench, hinting he wanted to get on with his work. Then he put it down. "Does anybody else know she was pregnant, Julie? Have you told anyone?"

"No, Bernie, I couldn't – not until I'd told you. She said I could tell you."

"Why me?" He smiled, but his jaw tightened. The poisonous little bitch had been spreading hints. "That Barbara," he shook his head, "she had ... she *has* some funny ideas. Always romancing about something, isn't she?" He tried to get Julie to agree. "That's what she is, isn't she – a romancer?"

Julie nodded.

"I doubt if she really is pregnant, Julie, don't you? Not pregnant at all – just romancing. So I wouldn't say anything about it until she turns up – not a word to anybody. It would only get her into more trouble, now wouldn't it?"

"I suppose so, Bernie."

"And not so much of the Bernie, young lady." Playfully he waved the wrench at her. "I'm Mr Friend to you – as I always was to your friend."

"But Bernie…"

"And not a word to anyone until she turns up." He walked with her to the door. "Not a word, young lady, or you'll have Mr Friend to answer to."

He went back, still clutching the wrench. It was very clean in his oily hands. Too clean. He had burnished it too thoroughly, using a blowtorch on it, burning off every trace that may have stuck to it. Washing would have been useless. Particles always lodged in waste pipes and drains, and could be found. Burning was the only way. But he had made it too clean; no garage man had a wrench as spotless as this. Bernard Friend dropped it on the floor and trod on it.

In The Doves that night he criticized the police. "One of our young girls goes missing," he said, "and they're not doing a blind thing."

"Pound to a penny she's in London," said the landlord.

"With some young feller," said Bernie.

"I reckon Bernie wishes it was him," said someone else, and there was a laugh.

Bernard Friend's pint was half-way to his

mouth, but he put it back on the bar and stood for a moment gazing at the floor. "In the circumstances," he said, raising his head as if from prayer, "that isn't a very funny remark. I always found her a very pleasant young lady."

"But she was just ready for it, wasn't she, that one? You must've known it, Bernie. Waltzing past your place, flaunting it."

Bernie made no response and shamed the bar into silence. He took a drink, and said, "There ought to be a search – a really big search."

His earnestness was genuine, and it showed. He wanted a search – he needed a search around the village, every nook and cranny. It could only be then, after the search was over, that he would be able to bring the breakdown truck back to his yard. He couldn't have it standing there while police dogs sniffed around it. And time was running out. That truck had to be in his yard by tomorrow.

"If the police aren't going to do anything," he said, "we ought to organize our own search parties."

"That's right, Bernie," they agreed, but as it happened the police were ahead of him. The first parties were out early the next morning, and it was Bernard Friend himself who suggested that the search should begin in his scrapyard.

"You never know what kids might get up to," he said, and he watched the dogs nosing among the piles of old cars as he stood by with a crowbar to jemmy open locked boots.

Nothing was found, but then he turned to a tumbledown lean-to built against the back wall of his garage. "As I told your officer, I'm tidying this place up a bit," he said to the inspector. "So that old shed has got to come down. OK if I go ahead?"

"I don't see why not, Mr Friend."

"Everyone calls me Bernie, inspector – even the kids sometimes." It was a bit of insurance, just in case Julie said something. "Cheeky young devils."

"It's the way they've been brought up," said the inspector. "They're not like we were."

"They're not all bad." Bernie took a breath. "As a matter of fact I'm going to use that old shed to give them a bit of a treat."

"How's that, Bernie?"

His name, coming from beneath a peaked cap, was an intimacy that he did not, after all, care for, but he managed to smile. "Guy Fawkes night tomorrow," he said, "so I thought I'd use the timber to give 'em a good old bonfire on my paddock." He pointed to rough ground alongside the heaped cars. "Maybe it'll help to take their minds off this ghastly business."

"It's not ghastly yet, Bernie. She could still turn up."

"Of course, of course." He looked up at the eyes half hidden in the shadow of the cap. "I just keep thinking you're going to find her somewhere … find her, you know…"

"Dead?" said the inspector. "That remains to be seen." He turned away. "Watch how you go, Bernie."

Bernie knew that the bonfire was a stroke of genius. When Barbara's body had first sagged against him and he had lowered her to the floor of his office, his first impulse had been to take her miles away and bury her.

He had even rolled her in the strip of old carpet pulled from under his desk, but then, as he lifted her to carry her out to the boot of his car, he had suddenly realized what he was doing. He was acting as if he was in a movie. The roll of carpet, the car boot, the scraped grave. He had seen it many times. And every real-life murderer did the same. They copied the movies. And if there was a pattern for murderers, there was also a pattern for the police. They knew where to look.

So he had left her on his office floor while he backed his breakdown truck into the garage. Then he emptied the tool chest behind the cab. It was cramped, but Barbara was not a large girl and he got her in. Then he padlocked the chest and, for extra safety, put spot welds at the corners of the lid, disguising their newness with dirt.

By the time he had loaded a scooter into the back it was dark, and it was unlikely that anyone had seen him drive out of the village. Eight miles away, in town, he parked in the yard behind a garage he often did business with. They would think nothing of it. Then he rode the scooter home.

The truck was still miles away when Bernard Friend took the morning off to help in the fruitless search. In the afternoon he began to pull down the shed and build the bonfire in the middle of his paddock. Several kids came to help him, Julie among them, but her mind wasn't on it. Every now and again she would stand still and look around.

"Come on, Julie," he called. "We'll never get done at this rate."

"I just wish I knew something," she said. "I just wish I knew where she was."

One of the mothers came into the paddock and Bernie went up to her. "I thought this would take their minds off things," he said. "Keep them active and stop them moping."

She looked apprehensively at the pile of wood. "It's going to be very big, isn't it, Mr Friend?"

"Might as well give them a good time," he said, and smiled sadly. Then a group tilting a roof beam against the heap caught his eye and he broke off to tell them to be careful. "Young tearaways," he said, "but don't worry, they're safe with me."

"You're very good to think of all this, Mr Friend."

"I'm doing myself a service at the same time." He grinned broadly, feeling suddenly on top of his problem. "There's too much old rubbish lying around, I must admit, so everybody's going to be pleased with good old Bernie when it's done."

He was still smiling to himself when he helped Julie roll an old tyre up the slope of the paddock. He had constructed a tunnel of tyres in the centre of the bonfire and was still adding to it. Julie stooped to gaze inside.

"It's dark in there, Bernie," she said.

"Mr Friend," he corrected her.

"Yeh, Mr Friend." She looked sideways at him.

"That's better, Julie. Show a little respect to your elders."

Suddenly her eyes filled with tears. "I hope some

little kid doesn't get in there to hide. That would be terrible."

"Julie, Julie," he said. "Cheer up. Can you see a caring person like myself letting that happen?"

"I was just thinking that Barbara might want a place like that to shelter, Bern … I mean Mr Friend. Suppose she's hurt herself and is lying out there in the woods somewhere."

He carefully did not put his hand on her shoulder, and he raised his voice so that all the helpers could hear. "I'm quite sure Barbara is safe, Julie. Wherever she is. Somebody is taking good care of her – very good care." He covered the mouth of the tunnel and put more timber over it. "Nothing can get in there now, Julie. Not a living soul."

Julie gave him a watery smile. "You make me feel a lot better, Mr Friend," she said.

"Good girl."

It was late before the bonfire was finished, and later still before Bernard Friend rode his scooter over to town. The breakdown truck stood behind the garage in the darkness. He had a story ready, a towing job he had to do next day, but the garage was closed and nobody spoke to him or, he was certain, even saw him.

A light drizzle was falling as he put a strap around his scooter and used the breakdown crane to crank it into the back of the truck. It clanked suddenly against the tool chest. "Sorry," he said, and for the first time realized that a dead girl lay curled up within inches of him. He had been so busy he had not even checked the lid of the chest. He looked carefully around the yard. There were

23

parked vehicles everywhere and many shadows, but nothing moved. Even then he gave the lid only a quick glance and tugged at it once. Nobody had interfered. It was shut tight.

Bernard Friend was whistling as he drove out of the yard. Even the drizzle lifted.

It was very late that night when a bright light flickered briefly in his garage and the welds that held the tool chest lid were cut through. Tarpaulins shrouded the truck as he lifted the lid, and soon afterwards the last glimmer of light went out in the garage and the whole village was dark and still under the stars.

Minutes went silently by before, very slowly, a shadow detached itself from the darkened garage and moved towards the open ground of the paddock. The shadow was broad, made broader by the bulk of something it cradled in its arms, but Bernard Friend had powerful muscles and moved lightly despite the weight. The only sound was the breath in his nostrils, like some night-wandering animal snuffling for food.

He lowered his burden and looked around. The dark trees collected extra shadows to shroud the hillside above him, and the stars pricked the empty sky like the frost that was beginning to whiten the grass. The pyramid of the bonfire was a tent where, cautiously, he drew back the doorflap of old timbers and revealed the deeper blackness of the tunnel inside. Stiffened by its roll of carpet, the body slid into its tomb.

Bernard Friend piled extra wood over the entrance and made one more journey to pour sump oil into the centre of the pyre before he drew back and left the frost to crystallize over his footprints.

Nothing now to do but wait and watch. The thought had occurred to him that he might make the bonfire blaze tonight and blame it on spoil-sport youths, but surely someone, some busybody aroused by the flames, would then make an attempt to put it out. No, he would keep watch. Then there would be no risk.

Nevertheless it was going to be a cold night. His bungalow was behind the garage, out of sight of the paddock, so he had to keep watch from the workshop.

He put on extra clothes, but still he shivered. And all because of that stupid Barbara kid. She had said she wasn't going to get pregnant … she had promised him over and over … and then she had let it happen. And she'd been proud of it.

His fists clenched as if they once again held the wrench. She should never have told him – not just at that moment, not smiling, not pretending she'd done something clever. Anger licked through him again. She'd asked for it. His fist hit the bench … with the same short, powerful jab that had brought the wrench down across her stupid smile.

He grunted and leant forward to rub the dirty window pane. Nothing stirred outside. The bonfire was neat and high. He was a good mechanic, everyone said so, and this was a job well done. He thought it through again. Nothing would go wrong. He was so certain of it that he was dozing when the first light dimmed the stars, but nothing had disturbed the dark pyramid.

Once during the day he came outside after answering the telephone to find kids piling new rubbish on the bonfire. He had yelled at them before he'd had time to think, but at least it had made them leave him alone until late afternoon. Then Julie came up to him.

"Bernie," she said, "I mean Mr Friend. Sorry."

"That's all right, Julie." He smiled at her. She stood in front of him in the forlorn way she'd always had. Barbara had been the dominant one, had bullied her and sent her away whenever she'd wanted to be alone with Bernie in his office. Which was often enough. He'd miss it. "What is it, Julie?" he asked.

"Everybody wants to know what time we're going to start." She smiled at him. "They're ever so keen."

He glanced out through the garage door. The sun was already behind the hill, and he could not delay much longer. But suddenly he feared what the flames might show. He had to have time to pile on more wood. "How about seven?"

"That's too late," she whined.

Shut up. The words were in his mind but they stayed inside him. Ridges showed in his cheeks. Shut up, or you'll join your stupid friend. When he did speak he kept his voice calm. "I keep putting it off in case Barbara turns up," he said.

Again the moisture in her eyes. "I wish I knew where she was. Haven't you any idea at all, Mr Friend?"

"Julie." His voice rumbled towards her. "How old are you, Julie?"

"Sixteen," she said.

Then stop behaving like a kid of twelve, he yelled in silence behind his teeth. Aloud, he said, "Well, I'll put you in charge, Julie. Tell them I won't have anybody here before half past six." He realized he had to make more torches so that every point should be touched with flame and no dead patches could show what lay there.

"Thanks ever so much, Mr Friend," and she turned away. His hatred burned at her back as his eyes watched her leave the yard.

They were early, as he knew they would be, but he was ready for them. The torches touched, and the smoke went up into a clear sky. But all was not well. The flames burned sullenly as if reluctant to advance into the dark heart of the pyramid. And faces, flickering in the uncertain firelight, ringed the paddock, observing every detail.

A boy advanced and poked at one of the dwindling firespots with a stick.

"Stop jabbing at it!" Bernie snatched the stick, and the boy backed away, startled. "I'm the only one who can make it go. Stand clear – all of you!" He ran into the garage and came back carrying a can.

It was a dangerous mixture that Bernard Friend flung at the smouldering wood. In an instant flames whirled in a spiral and bit deep with a roar that flung forked leaves of fire at the timbers and tossed the white petals of an enormous flower high into the sky. And the heat, pressing on uncovered skin, pushed everyone back.

"She's away!" shouted the boys, and soon rockets

flew to burst among the stars, and girls screamed as crackers exploded in the grass.

Many eyes watched the flames, but none so closely as Bernie's. The heart of the bonfire had become a blazing city where red towers of glowing wood were eaten away in the heat and collapsed into the scorching alleyways. Blue flames, so hot they were all but invisible, danced like devils in the streets, and white fragments, lighter than snow-flakes, broke free and rode the hurricane that, feeding on itself, peeled layer after layer from the silent, waiting depth of the heap.

The tyres showed. Bernie risked the heat to throw fallen wood towards them. Their black rubber bub-bled and sent out smoke so dense it made shadows even inside the glare of the blaze until, unable to resist it for a moment longer, the smoke lost its blackness and was transformed into greasy flame.

Julie saw Mr Friend's face, always so broad and brown and now reddened by fire, take on a new shade. A paleness, in spite of the heat, seemed to shine there, and she was watching him and not the blaze when the first tyre split open.

His lips had parted, and his strong white teeth shone whiter, but his eyes had narrowed and pierced the flames. She turned away from him to see what held him so fast.

What she saw was a roar of blue emptiness under the arch of the gaping tunnel, and on its floor a shapeless shape lying there, a flaking, shrinking, dwindling darkness in the heart of it all. But at that moment the bonfire collapsed inwards in a firestorm of such intensity that it sucked the

28

oxygen out of the November night and made the watchers reel back, gasping for breath.

She turned to Mr Friend, wanting to ask what it was that she had seen, but now he was circling the blaze, stooping to throw every scrap of wood towards the centre. He never stopped. He was still doing it when the last firework had punctured the sky, and the last straggler had left for home.

Julie was the last of all. She had left the paddock and was turning the corner of the garage when the thought of Barbara tugged suddenly at her heart and she knew she had to ask if, somewhere among the hills, Barbara could have seen the bonfire at this moment and might have been dragging herself towards it. She turned back.

Bernard Friend was silhouetted against the mound of red embers. He was raking into it, stirring up chrysanthemums of sparks. He did not hear her as she approached over the trodden grass.

"Bernie," she said softly.

He stopped his raking, listening, not sure where the voice came from.

"Bernie," she said again, and he looked over his shoulder.

Julie could not see his face. All she was aware of was that he dropped his rake and backed away from her, skirting the edges of the fire, putting it between her and himself. Now, with the glowing heap between them, his face became visible. She could not account for the fear that pulled down the corners of his mouth.

"It's only me, Bernie," she said, and took a step forward. It was then that she saw what it was that

29

terrified him. It was the bonfire, the mound of redness.

Bernie knew it had consumed everything. Every atom. He knew no trace of Barbara remained. And no trace was ever found, but that night, under the stars, the dying bonfire rustled and stirred.

Julie saw the embers heave in just one place, as though the red heap had become brown, cool earth and some small animal burrowed there. The glowing ashes turned again and then, from the centre, there arose a small entity, a little shape of fire. It had a small torso, small limbs, and a head of flame. And it walked.

Bernard Friend was caught against the fence. He tried to shuffle sideways, but his clothes snagged on the wire and he was held in a crouch. He struggled, but the wire bit deeper and he was still crouching when the little figure, clothed in heat, trod unsteadily towards him.

Julie saw Bernard Friend slip and fall. He sat with his back against the fence, and she saw the burning baby come up to him, hold out its arms and wriggle into his lap.

Bernard Friend had made sure that his working overalls showed the mark of his trade; oil had soaked into them. And now, at the baby's touch, flames ran along his legs and arms and sat on his shoulders like wings. He was drenched in fire.

He cried out, but the fire had reached his lungs and the scream that came forth was made visible. It was a torch, a gush of flame from his blistering lips. The whole village heard it, but only one saw it.

Julie watched, and Bernie burned.

UNDER THE ICE

Very few people have actually seen a ghost. I have. But I wish I hadn't.

Rupert saw it long before I did, and I was the only person he ever told about it. I just wish he'd kept quiet, and then things might have turned out differently – at least I wouldn't have been there on that terrible day and I would never have seen what I did see. And I would never have known how unfair it was. There was no justice in it. None.

I have often thought I could have done something to stop it – but now I know that was impossible; I couldn't have done a thing. I'm only telling you this because I can't keep it to myself any longer.

I suppose you'd expect anybody who'd seen a ghost to tell everyone about it. Rupert was different. He kept things to himself. Quite a lot of people are like that, out in the flat fens. He had nobody much to talk to, so he got out of the habit, even with me, and I was always reckoned to be his best friend. He was a thin, gangly sort of boy, a bit taller than me, and he was tough in all sorts of ways you'd never guess just by looking at him.

I knew something was bothering him, but I didn't know what, although it had to be pretty important because one day, out of the blue, he asked me if I'd go home with him after school. It was a half holiday, in the middle of a bitter winter, and I didn't fancy cycling such a long way.

"It'll be dark before long," I said, trying to make an excuse.

"That doesn't matter," he said in a rush. "My father will take us, and we can go skating. There's no danger, the ice is rock hard... So that'll be all right, will it?"

"Hold your hosses," I said. This wasn't like Rupert at all, the quiet boy from far out of town. "What am I going to do with my bike?" I wasn't going to leave that in the cycle shed all night, not with some of the characters I knew hanging about. "And what about my tea – my mum'll be expecting me."

"I'll give you some tea," he said, just as if he owned the whole house, the bread and butter and everything. "Give your mum a ring – and you can put your bike in the boot." His father had a Volvo like a battle tank, so that was OK.

"Skates," I said. "I haven't got any." My lovely brother in the sixth form nicked everything that belonged to me. "William's screwed my skates on to his boots," I told Rupert, "so what's the use?"

"How big are your feet?" he said suddenly.

"Not as big as his."

"Same size as me." He plonked his foot down next to mine. "You can have my old fen runners."

"Gee," I said. "Thanks a million."

He went red. "Or you can have my Norwegians. I don't mind."

"Don't worry about it, Rupe." I was beginning

to feel sorry for him; he seemed so eager for me to go with him that it would have been just like disappointing a little kid if I'd said no. So I said yes. You never do know what you're letting yourself in for.

He was in a fidget waiting for his father after school and he didn't calm down until we'd stowed the bike and were sitting side by side in the back seat. You could have told it was a farmer's car by the old fertilizer sacks in the boot, but even the back of his father's neck would have let you into the secret because it was brown and creased, and the trilby hat he wore was a mud colour through always being out in the sun and rain. I used to get on with his father quite well, chatting about this and that, but I hadn't seen him for some time, and now he was like Rupert – so quiet that after a while I began to feel as if he was some sort of servant in the front seat, just doing his job by driving us home. This made me so awkward that I kept silent, too.

Rupert practically ignored me. He sat back in his corner and gazed out of the window with his mind on something else while the heater blew warm air at us and I began to wish I was at home by the fire. If I'd had any sense I would have stopped feeling sorry for myself and would have remembered what it was that kept them so subdued. Everybody knew what had happened last summer, but that afternoon it just didn't come into my mind.

It had been freezing for a week so I was used to a nip in the air when I was cycling home, but when we got to where Rupert lived and stepped out of the car the cold was something else. In town it lay in chunks like massive ice cubes between the houses and you felt you could dodge some of it, but out here, where there were no streets and no street lights, the cold was a solid black mass that seemed to press even the birds to the ground.

"Don't know what there is to eat," said Rupert's father. "Bread and pull-it, I reckon." I couldn't tell if he smiled because he turned his head away, but I guessed he didn't bother. "The wife wasn't expecting anyone."

Nice welcome, I thought, but I was polite. "I don't mind, Mr Granger," I said. "I'm not very hungry."

"That's all right, then," and he left us, striding away over the crackling gravel to the farm out-buildings.

"I don't think I should've come," I said, but Rupert was already taking me past the frozen bushes to the back door.

He went ahead of me, and the instant the door opened his mother gave a little cry and called out "Who's there?" as if we were burglars. Even when Rupert told her it was just the two of us she kept peering over his shoulder to make sure exactly who was following him out of the shadows.

"It's only me," I said.

"Oh," she said, and some of the alarm went out of her eyes, but the worry remained. "David Maxey. What are you doing here?"

This time even Rupert could tell I wasn't being given a very warm welcome, and he was embarrassed. "He's hungry," he said.

"But you never said you were bringing anyone."
She was quite bitchy with him. "You never told
me."

I butted in. "I'm sorry, Mrs Granger," I said, and
wished more strongly than ever to be somewhere
else. "It's Rupert's fault. He wants me to go skating."

"Skating?" The idea seemed to confuse her.

"Mother." Rupert went close to her. "You know
you don't like me to go skating on my own – so
that's why I brought him. Two together are quite
safe."

She was looking from one to the other of us, and
I said, "If she cracks she bears, if she bends she
breaks." It was something they said about the ice
in the fens, where everybody was a skater and
knew about such things. "It's very thick now, Mrs
Granger, and it'll never bend an inch."

She didn't answer. Instead, she turned to the
dresser and took down plates to set a new place for
me. "I'm afraid there's not much," she said.

I'd always liked Rupert's mother. She'd never
seemed as if she belonged out here, miles from anywhere, with no neighbours. It was partly the way
she dressed I suppose, as if she was ready to leave
the farm behind at that instant and take us both up
to town for a good time. But now there wasn't a
trace of make-up on her face, and the shadows
around her eyes were genuine.

"I'll get the skates," said Rupert. "They're in the
garage."

I didn't want him to leave me, but I made the
best of it by trying to help his mother. There wasn't

as much on the table as I was used to when I went there, and she apologized. "I haven't been able to get out to the shops in this weather," she said. It wasn't true; there hadn't been enough snow to make the roads dangerous, and I knew she had her own car.

"This is fine, Mrs Granger," I said. "I can hardly eat a thing."

At any other time she would have seen through the lie and laughed; now she just turned towards me, her face full of anxiety, and said, "Are you sure? Are you really sure?"

I'd always thought that, as mothers go, she was rather pretty, and I was so shocked at how pale and lined her face had become that I found I had no words, and I was very relieved when Rupert returned with the fen runners for me. The little skates, which were like the blades of table knives set in blocks of wood, were those he'd started with when he was younger. The boots were tight, but I managed to squeeze my feet into them.

Dusk was beginning to fall by the time we'd eaten and left the house. Mrs Granger stood at the door with her hands clenched in front of her as if she had to struggle not to reach out and hold us back.

"The ice is rock hard, Mrs Granger," I said, making a new attempt to stop her worrying. "We couldn't go through it even if we tried."

"Don't," she said, "please don't say things like that." She looked around the yard. "Rupert, why don't you get your father to go with you?"

But Rupert was already walking away and his

father, who had not joined us at tea, was nowhere to be seen.

I'd always known that the farmhouse was lonely, but I'd never realized just how isolated it really was until I caught up with Rupert on the road outside. In summer, green trees and bushes and tall grass crowded around the house and disguised its loneliness, but now the curtains of leaves had been stripped away, and the flat fields, the black furrows ridged with white, stretched away like the bare boards of an empty house.

"Cold," I said, and the blades of the skates that swung in our hands rattled like chattering teeth.

The proper road petered out just beyond the farmhouse and became a track that only tractors could use. There were no hedges out here, only ditches with thin crusts of ice where the water had seeped away beneath. I would have stopped to throw stones through the ice sheets except that Rupert was hurrying ahead, intent on getting somewhere – even though there seemed to be no place better than any other out here.

"It's getting dark early," he said. "It's all this cloud. You won't be able to see it soon."

"See what?" I asked, but he had run on as if he didn't want to answer.

We came to a gate across the track and beyond it a low bank stretched away to left and right like the rampart of an ancient fort. On the other side lay the waterway, except that now it was an iceway, reaching in a dead straight line to the black horizon.

"When there's a moon," said Rupert, "you can skate out of sight."

Our voices were so small in the vast space that I doubt if they reached the far bank of the wide channel, not that there was anybody in the whole of creation to hear us. An ice age had made the world a waste land, and we were alone in it.

"Where are you taking me?" I asked, because I'd guessed by now that he had something more than skating on his mind.

"Hurry up and get those runners on," he said, and he had laced up his Norwegians and was crabbing down the bank almost before I'd started. I heard his long blades strike the ice as I still struggled with my laces. "Wait for me," I called, because he was already gliding out from the bank.

"Hurry up. It's getting dark."

He was out in the middle of the channel when I reached the edge, caught the tip of one skate in a tussock of frozen grass and stumbled forward. I was sure I was going to get a wet foot in the seepage that is always at the margin, but my blades ran through the grass on solid ice. It was as hard as a marble floor from bank to bank. There was no risk of falling through; none at all – but Rupert was leading me on to a danger that was much worse.

We skated, sawing the air with our arms and feeling it bite back at our cheeks and noses, but he, riding high on blades twice the length of mine, easily outpaced me, and I was so far behind that there must have been a hundred metres of ice between us when I saw him circling, waiting for me to catch up.

I was a breathless plodder following a racehorse, and I had lost patience with him so I deliberately dawdled, bending low from time to time, merely letting myself slide slowly along. It must have been infuriating for him, but he gave no sign of it, and continued to cut his slow circles as I drifted closer.

"We don't need a moon," I called. "You can still see for miles." The scatter of snow had made the banks white enough to catch all the thin light that came from the sky and we stood out like dark birds gliding low over frozen fields. But what food would birds find out here? What could they peck at? I was soon to find out.

"I'm flying!" I cried, and I leant forward and spread my arms wide. He had stopped and was waiting for me, and I wondered if I could reach him without pushing again, so I allowed myself to glide.

I was looking down, watching the little blades of the fen runners barely rocking as they skimmed forward, and I realized how smooth the ice was. It was a glassy pavement, polished, without cracks or blemishes, and it came as a shock to see that it was so clear I was actually looking through it. Even in this light I could see into the dark water below, where I knew the long weeds trailed in summer, and I gazed down into a giddy blackness.

My glide had been so successful that I was laughing as my skates came to rest almost at Rupert's feet, and I was just about to raise my head when I caught a glimpse of something beneath the ice. At first I thought it was a twist of weed, and I stooped to look closer. The shape became clear, and in that instant it reached inside me with a sick coldness that held me fixed to the spot. And then, horrified, not wanting to touch the ice anywhere near what I had seen, I eased myself backwards, still crouching, and stood up.

It was only then that I raised my eyes to Rupert.

There was a bridge behind him, in the distance. It was a single span where the track from the farm crossed the channel, and I remember it because it made a black shadow on a level with his shoulders and he seemed for an instant to have enormous arms that stretched from bank to bank. At that awful moment even he terrified me, and I was beginning to draw further back, when he spoke.

"So you can see it, too." The words were like frost on his lips.

I nodded. I saw it clearly. There was a drowned man under the ice.

I could see the folds of his trousers and a shoe twisted at an awkward angle. The sleeves of his jacket were rigid, but his fingers seemed to lie at ease in the ice, resting, as plump and white as the flesh of a plucked chicken. His head was turned away from us, so all we saw was hair and one ear.

I said something, but I can't remember what. All I knew was that we had to go for help even if it was too late – we had to let someone know. That object locked beneath us had to be freed. Words came from me, but Rupert did nothing. He stood quite still.

"Look again," he said.

I turned my eyes to the ice between us but I must have drifted too far back because now I could see nothing. I edged forward. The ice was black, and empty. I cast around, stooping to peer closer, but nothing showed itself.

"Where is it?" I said. The hideous thought came to my mind that a current still flowed under the ice and that the man was rolling slowly beneath our feet. "Where is it now?" I was beginning to panic, taking timid steps on my skates away from the spot as if the ice were about to open and take me down to join the corpse in its frozen coffin. "Where?" I said. "Where?"

"It's still there." His voice was so flat and calm it made me jerk my head up. "It's my uncle," he said.

He skated slowly forward. The extra height of his Norwegians made him tower over me, and once again I was afraid of him. His uncle! He had seen his uncle dead under the ice, and now he was gliding towards me without a sign of grief or even surprise on his face. I was backing clumsily away when he came level with me, and a thin smile appeared on his lips.

"You're not thinking of skating backwards all the way home, are you?" he said.

The fact that he could say something so ordinary, and smile as he spoke, jolted me out of my panic. I even managed to shrug. "How can it be your uncle?" I began ... and then I remembered. It all came flooding back to me, and at the same instant I knew why his mother was so haggard and his father so silent. The tragedy that had slipped from my mind was still strong within them.

"Oh," I said feebly, "your uncle."

And then my stomach turned over yet again, for his uncle had been dead many months, drowned out here in the fens.

"That was where it happened," Rupert said. "Last summer."

I was ashamed of myself for having forgotten, and for a moment this blotted everything else from my mind. "I'm sorry," I said. "I should have remembered."

"I was there when he was found." He began to move away. "That's how I know who it is in the ice."

So there really was a body there ... but he was talking nonsense to say it was his uncle. "It can't be," I said. "It's just some old clothes."

"With fingers?"

"Well, it's another body." I didn't want to admit it. "Someone else. We've got to tell somebody. We've got to."

He said nothing. He moved away and I went with him. Our skates were silent and we drifted like ghosts through the bitter dusk. I twisted my head to look behind.

"There's nothing to see," he said. "Even if you go back you won't find it. It's gone."

"How do you know?"

He turned a gaunt face towards me, and once again he smiled. "Do you think I haven't tried?"

"But I saw it. If I can see it, so can somebody else. Have you tried to show anybody?"

Suddenly, as though we were racing, he lowered his head and stretched his legs in long, sweeping strokes that left me behind. I did not catch up with him until we reached the place where we had left our shoes. He was already crouching on the bank unlacing his boots. "Too late to go any further," he said. "Too dark."

We had just seen something impossible to explain, and that was all he had to say.

"It was a ghost," I said, "wasn't it?" And when that had no effect on him, I added, "Or a shadow or something. Some sort of cracks and bubbles in the ice. The light might just catch them at times." He remained silent, but I wasn't going to leave it there. "You ought to tell somebody about it," I said. "Why not your mother?"

"She's got too much on her mind." He concentrated on his laces for a while, and then, speaking so low I could hardly hear him, he said, "She liked my uncle. She liked him a lot."

"Well, you've got to speak to your father – you've got to tell him."

"I can't." He shook his head without looking up. "I can't." His fingers ceased fumbling with his laces but his head remained bowed, and after a while I saw his shoulders tremble and I realized he was crying.

We were side by side in the frozen grass and Rupert had bent his head to his knees and was sobbing like a little child. I had never seen him in tears; and now that it had happened, I did not know what to do. I began unfastening my own skates, waiting until his sobbing subsided, trying to think of something to say, and failing. His grief was too deep for me to reach. Then, suddenly, he raised his head and was once again speaking clearly.

"He hated him," he said. "My father hated him. They used to be friends and then he hated him."

"But they were brothers."

"What difference does that make?" His voice

45

was harsh. "He liked my mother! My uncle liked my mother, didn't he? A lot. Too much. I heard him say so, didn't I?"

He spat the words at me so fiercely I had to face up to him. "I don't know what you heard," I said.

"I heard everything!" He sucked in his cheeks and glared at me as though I was the most detestable creature on earth. "My father said he'd kill him if he didn't go away. Kill him!" He stooped forward suddenly and hauled off his skates. "Now you can go home," he said. "Get lost!"

Neither of us said another word. I climbed the bank alone and got to his house ahead of him. I could see his mother and father through the kitchen window, but I didn't go in. I was in a hurry to get away from that place, so I found my bike and left.

The freeze got worse. Rupert and I saw each other at school and were still friends, but we never once mentioned what had happened. His outburst seemed to have shut the door on it, and there was a kind of haughtiness in him that made me see that he was so deeply ashamed of what he had told me he could never speak of it. I told myself that what I had seen in the ice was made by weeds frozen near the surface, and that it was Rupert's imagination, because of the terrible time he'd been through that had somehow forced us both to see what he'd seen last summer when they found his uncle.

Then one day the sun shone. The clouds, that for weeks had ground their way towards the horizon as slowly as a glacier, showed gaps of blue, and the sun began to put its fingers through the thin crust of snow on gardens and gutters. Even Rupert smiled and said, "We shan't get much more skating this year, I reckon."

"Too bad," I replied, thinking that he wanted to shrug the whole business away for ever.

"So why don't you come over tomorrow before it's too late?" he asked.

He had taken me by surprise and I looked so sharply at him that he reddened and mumbled something, saying that there were bound to be other people around as it was a Saturday, so there was nothing to worry about. It was the nearest he'd come to mentioning what was on our minds, and I was a bit nettled that he thought I may have been afraid to go skating alone out there, so of course I said yes.

I even managed to get my skates from my brother, so I was properly equipped when I cycled out to see him. The sun was bright, but I had to push against a biting wind which kept the temperature so low that I knew the ice would still be in good condition. And Rupert was right about other people being there. You could never say the ice was crowded because there was so much of it, but there were skaters wherever you looked, and their tiny black figures were dotted away into the distance. An occasional speed man came slicing by, one arm behind his back and the other swinging, and we decided we would join these long-distance skimmers.

Without either of us saying a word we set out towards the distant bridge and this meant we had to go over the spot where the shadows had frightened us so badly. We did not ignore it, but neither did we linger. We circled once, gazing down, and I was certain of the exact spot because the ice there was clear even though its surface was now criss-crossed by blade strokes. The sunlight would have shown any dead man beneath the ice, but there was nothing. There was only darkness below, and when I looked up and caught Rupert's eye he grinned sheepishly and skated off at speed as if to put it behind him once and for all.

We could hear the squeals of girls and the shouts of boys long before we reached the little groups that were strung out over the ice, but we skimmed by until we were far out in the fens. The sun, although now a blazing red, had shed the last of its heat for the day and was beginning to bury itself in the horizon before we thought of turning back. We stretched out on the frozen grass for a few minutes to rest our ankles.

"It's good out here," said Rupert. He was panting and there was even some colour in his cheeks. "I'm glad you could come today."

We weren't in the habit of paying each other compliments, so I just mumbled that I, too, was enjoying myself. I expected the matter to end there, but Rupert had something on his mind; unfinished business.

"Sorry I was such an idiot last time," he said.

"That's OK." I didn't look at him.

"It's just that everything was getting on top of me – Mum and Dad not being very happy and all that. Things had just been getting worse and worse, ever since..."

He seemed to want me to say it for him.

"I know what you mean," I said, but that wasn't good enough for him; he wanted it out in the open.

"Since my uncle drowned himself." He spoke very clearly, forcing me to look at him. "Drowned himself," he repeated. "I told you something stupid about my dad last time. It wasn't true."

"I know it wasn't." I had to agree with him. His father could never had done such a terrible thing as murder his brother, no matter what he might have said. "You were feeling pretty bad," I told Rupert. "And we'd just seen that thing in the ice."

"*Thought* we'd seen. It's not there now."

"And it wasn't there then," I insisted, backing him up. "It was just imagination. By both of us."

"Both of us." He nodded. He was glad he had a friend, and to know that between us we'd scattered all the shadows from his mind. "Right," he said, "I'll race you back."

It was no race. He had done much more skating than me and his ankles were stronger, so from time to time he had to wait for me to catch up. We had gone further out into the fen than I had realized and, with my slow progress, the sun had dipped below the horizon and had left only an afterglow before the bridge came in sight.

We were alone, the other skaters having long since climbed the banks and gone home, so when we came up to the bridge it was our voices alone that echoed beneath it.

"One at a time," said Rupert. "The thaw has made it wet under there."

He went first. There was no suggestion of a

crack as he went forward cautiously, but when I followed I could see that his weight had made a pulse of water spill from the edge, so I kept to the centre as he waited for me to come through.

I was concentrating so intensely on the ice beneath my skates that I almost ran into him and had to make a wide swerve to keep my balance. That was why I saw his father before he did. Mr Granger was at the top of the bank, looking down.

"Where have you been?" he called to Rupert. "Your mother was worried."

Rupert did not answer. He was leaning forward like a runner trying to get his breath, and I went up alongside him to taunt him. He did not even turn his head my way and I was stooping to look into his face when I saw that, although his mouth was open, he was not gasping for breath. He was in the grip of terror.

I did not wish to follow his gaze, but I was forced to turn my head and look down.

It was there. I saw the frozen shoe and trouser leg, the stiff folds of the jacket and the fingers cased in ice. Even the hair on the back of the twisted head was visible.

Neither Rupert nor I moved. We were locked to that dreadful place.

"What are you doing down there?" It was his father's voice from the bank. "It's time to go home."

I had my hand on Rupert's arm. I was beginning to pull him back, gently tugging at him, and my skates were making a faint rasping sound on the ice when it happened. The head began to turn. It was as though I had been scratching at the other side of a window pane and had aroused it. The head within the ice came round to face us. Yellow cheeks and an open mouth. And then the eyes, tight shut.

"What's happening?" Mr Granger's voice died and, as it did so, leaving the air empty of all sound, the eyelids lifted. A handspan of ice lay over them, but the eyelids slipped back like a flicker of moonlight, and a pair of dead eyes, grey and as pale as milk, stared up at us.

The cold air brushed the back of my neck as I jerked backwards, but Rupert did not stir. He remained where he was as the fingers came through the ice, and with them, the bulge of the head. It came up like a sleeper pushing back a sheet.

I heard Rupert's name shouted from the top of the bank, and his father came thudding and slithering towards him and snatched him away.

I had slid backwards and was beneath the bridge when the dead figure stood upright and came to collect them. Water ran from its sleeves and dripped from its pale, plump fingers, and its sodden shoes swished on the ice as it advanced.

Without realizing it, I had backed even further away, out of the shelter of the bridge, so I was clear of what happened. I was a spectator ... as Rupert should have been. But he was with his father.

I saw them enter the shadow of the dark arch together, and I saw Rupert slip and fall full length. His father stooped for him, but never got a chance to lift his son upright. The dripping figure came mowing towards them and, in the black shadow under the bridge, embraced them both.

The impact of Rupert's fall had been too much for the ice. There was a soft, rending crack and a sheet the size of a table up-ended itself and in an instant, without a sound, the huddle of figures had gone. I flung myself forward, but the ice had slid back into place. I kicked it, but it was wedged. I put my full weight on its edge, and still it did not budge. I knelt and hammered on it, but Rupert was with his father on the other side of that door, and I never saw him again.

THE KEY

Sophie sat weeping in the rose garden. Martin, standing a few paces away, ground his feet deeper into the gravel and looked beyond the lawns to where the great Hall showed its face to the moon.

"I have the key," he said. "The Hall is all ours. Will you come with me, Sophie?"

"I can't." She bowed her head because she was ashamed to be weeping. "You know I can't."

Only a few hours ago, in the Gate House where Martin lived, they had overheard his parents talking about her. Mr and Mrs Medlicott were caretakers at the Hall, which was rarely in use, so their house was a lonely one, outside the village. Living alone seemed to have made them careless with doors, and their voices from two rooms away were quite clear.

"First girl he's ever brought to see his mum." Joe Medlicott was soft spoken, but even the clatter of plates from the kitchen where he was washing up did not drown his words. Sophie was shy. Her stomach shrank. "So what do you think of her?" said Joe.

Martin, alone with Sophie, snorted and went to close the door. He was not quick enough.

"She's a pretty girl," said Mrs Medlicott. "And I'll tell you something else … she's very keen on him."

Joe Medlicott was pleased. "He don't do so bad for a son of yours."

The door shut. "Old fool," said Martin.

Sophie, blushing, had to say something. "I like your father," she said, then realized it must seem she was agreeing with compliments, and her blush deepened. "I mean they're both nice." That only made it worse, but Martin had noticed nothing.

He suddenly said, "Do I look like him?"

"What do you mean?"

"It's simple enough... Do I look like him? Do I have his cow eyes, his bandy legs – his *sniff*?"

"Nothing like that." He had forced her into a comparison she did not want to make. But it was true he did not look like his father. He had his mother's fair colouring and narrow, handsome face. "You are more like your mother."

"Thank God for that."

"But he's still nice." She had to defend Joe Medlicott. She liked him; everybody did. But she had seen Martin watching him and hating the way he took very large bites when he ate and chewed very slowly, and she felt sorry for Joe. She made an attempt to deflect his son's attention. "Your mother is ever so sweet," she said.

"Sweet?" Martin had latched the door and was leaning against it. He suddenly seemed almost as tall as the doorpost, taller by far than Joe. "I wouldn't call her *sweet*, exactly. She's too intelligent to be merely sweet."

"Oh, but she's lovely to look at, Martin. Everybody says so."

"Too lovely, I guess. Too lovely for him, anyway."

The contempt in his voice warned her. He had led her into dangerous territory, and alarm made her say, "I don't know what you mean."

"Don't you?" He angled himself away from the door. "Most people down there," he nodded his head, indicating the village, "most of *them* would know what I mean."

She did not dare meet his eyes. Like everybody else she had heard talk about Mrs Medlicott. Sophie concentrated on the hands she was clenching in her lap, and tried to keep what people said out of her mind. But the knowledge was there. They said that Joe Medlicott might not have been Martin's father.

"If you're not going to speak, I may as well say it for you." Martin spoke deliberately, drawing out the words, insisting she should listen. "I thought everyone down there had heard the story about my mother."

"Why should I?" she burst out. "Why should I know! Why should I care!"

"Clive Millwood." His narrow face watched her like a fox. "Young Clive Millwood, the only son of the Millwoods up at the Hall – and my mother, a girl from the village. That's what the talk is about, isn't it?" He gave a sharp bark of laughter, and his eyes slanted as he smiled. "The young squire and a village girl. Who did they think they were – Romeo and Juliet?"

"I don't care! What difference does it make?"

"Oh, but it does. First it was Romeo and Juliet, and then there was me – Martin. Or should I be Clive? What do you think of Clive as a name?

Vastly superior to Martin, I think. But at least they didn't call me Joe – two Joe Medlicotts would be rather overstating the case."

"Don't say any more," Sophie begged. "Please. They might hear you."

"Does that matter?" His puzzled expression was false. "Am I saying something they don't know already?" Behind him the latch rattled, and he spun around to face Joe. Martin was unperturbed. "Hello, Father, we were just talking about you."

"I thought me ears was burning." Joe Medlicott's soft brown eyes were on Sophie. He smiled but said no more, and she gazed back at him, terrified at what might come next.

Martin suddenly sat himself on the arm of her chair. "My father has something of great importance to tell you," he said.

"That's news to me," said Joe Medlicott.

"He's been working up to it ever since you got here." Martin paused, and Sophie closed her eyes. "At any moment," Martin drawled, while Sophie's muscles stiffened, "my father will take you out and show you his garden."

Sophie had to struggle not to show her relief while Joe Medlicott, smiling broadly, shook his head. "He's got me weighed up, that boy," he said. "I can't keep track of him – he move far too fast for me, and that's a fact."

"Broad beans," said Martin. "They're a proper picture this year, isn't that a fact, Father?"

"Quite right, boy." Joe Medlicott seemed unaware that he was being mocked. "And that bean blossom have such a perfume it's a wonder people don't pick it for the house, ain't that so, Sophie?"

Mrs Medlicott had come to the door, and Sophie found herself agreeing with Martin; May Medlicott was too calm, too beautiful to be merely sweet. "Him and his bean blossom," she chided her husband. "I know something that she likes more than your old beans. Come with me, Sophie, and pick some lavender."

Martin shifted to let Sophie get to her feet. "That's the advantage of a large estate," he said. "Plenty of everything – even for the underlings."

May Medlicott held Sophie's arm. "He's got a sharp tongue," she said, "but he doesn't mean it – not all the time."

It was strange to pick lavender in the garden of the Gate House with May Medlicott; to know so much and yet say nothing. Sophie looked up the long avenue of trees towards the Hall, then glanced quickly and timidly at Martin's mother, afraid that even this would reveal what she knew of the past. But May Medlicott was stooping over the lavender bush, smiling to herself so placidly that Sophie longed to reach out and touch her and say that no matter what people said, she would never believe them.

"He doesn't like his mum and dad being caretakers, does he?" May Medlicott turned eyes that were as light a blue as Martin's towards her, and the smile was still on her face. "But it's a big job, Sophie, with the gardens and everything, and we were lucky to get it when we did. Joe and I were desperate to find a place, because Martin was on the way, and I think the Millwoods took pity on us."

Her openness was so astonishing that Sophie remained silent.

"Mind you," said May Medlicott, "I'd been quite friendly with young Clive Millwood." There was a hint of mischief in her face as she glanced at Sophie. "He was a strange boy. Frightening sometimes; you never knew where his moods were going to take him. But I got on well with him, so perhaps that helped."

Sophie busied herself with the lavender. She heard Martin's mother sigh.

"But then they went to live abroad," said May Medlicott, "because of what happened."

Because of what happened. The blood sang in Sophie's ears and she could not turn her eyes away from the woman who spoke so mildly of such huge events.

"It was a dreadful time." Martin's mother turned back to the lavender bush. "But it was so long ago that maybe people have forgotten." She handed some lavender heads to Sophie. "The Millwoods hardly ever come back," she said, "so we practically have the place to ourselves. Martin likes that."

It was dusk before Sophie walked with Martin through the grounds of the Hall to the rose garden.

"You had a long talk with my mother," he said. "Did she have anything interesting to say?"

"About what?"

"Oh, this and that." He tried to sound indifferent. "It's not important."

"Yes it is!" Sophie lost patience with him. "You're hinting all the time. Why can't you come out in the open with it?"

"That my father is not my father?"

"No! I don't believe what people say – and even if it's true I don't care!"

He must have detected something in her voice. "So she did say something," he said.

"But not that, Martin. I'm sure she didn't mean that. She would never have talked about Clive Millwood in the way she did if what people say had been true."

Martin laughed, disbelieving her. Exasperated, Sophie turned away, but he reached for her and held her arm.

"*You* may not believe what people say, Sophie, but there *is* one person who speaks the truth."

"Who's that?"

"My mother. She says Sophie Smith is the prettiest girl for miles and miles, and so she is."

Their lips had hardly touched when Sophie laughed and drew back. "Your father said it, too." She was conceited, she was flirting, and suddenly she had the confidence to speak. "I think everyone in the village is stupid to say things about your mother. You only have to talk to her to know that."

Martin no longer had his arms around her, and his face was cold in the moonlight. "You are telling me it's not true," he said.

"I know it isn't."

"Then why did Clive Millwood kill himself?"

Sophie had kept the suicide at the edge of her

mind. She had run from it. Now a door had shut and a bolt had shot home, and she was held in the depth of the dreadful time Martin's mother had spoken about. Clive Millwood had been found hanging. That was why the Millwoods had gone away and rarely came back; the house held too much pain for them.

"Why did he do it?" Martin insisted. "Why?"

Sophie cried out, "How would I know?"

"But I know." Martin looked at the ground, and his voice was no more than a murmur. "They wouldn't let him marry her. That's why he killed himself."

"No!" Her cry made his head jerk up. She gazed at him wildly, afraid of what she had to say. "He would have done it anyway!" Martin made no reply, but there was no going back. "That's the way he was. Your mother told me."

"My mother?"

Sophie said, "She was frightened of his moods. She told me so. But there was nothing else, Martin, no matter what anyone thinks. People put two and two together and get it wrong." She was leaning forward, trying to penetrate the shadows of his eyes as if she could make him see and hear May Medlicott. "It's not true, Martin. None of it is true."

For long seconds he gazed directly back at her, and then he smiled. "Pity," he said. "I would quite like to change my father." He was suddenly light-hearted. "But Joe wasn't wrong when he said I do all right for myself. I've got you, haven't I?"

"Yes," she said.

"Well, who cares about anything else?"

He snatched at her hand and ran with her along an avenue of tall trees, and they were out of breath when they stood on the lawn facing the Hall. In the moonlight its front was a cliff face slotted with crevices where birds could nest.

"Why are you shivering?" he asked.

"It's too big," said Sophie. "I could never live in that."

"You're cringing!" He was laughing. "Are you afraid of it?"

"I think so."

"Don't be so small!" He gripped her hand and they left the lawn and climbed the broad stone steps until they stood between the columns of the portico. "How can Sophie Smith be any less than anyone who ever lived here?" He took a key from his pocket and swung open one half of the huge door. "This place is ours."

She had no choice but to go with him. The vestibule was dark, but ahead of them a vast space opened out. He was about to swing the door shut behind them when she prevented him. "I don't want to be shut off," she said.

"From what?"

"From the open air. I don't like being in here."

"It's where I belong." He walked ahead, suddenly arrogant, challenging her to go with him. She advanced and they stood side by side on a marble floor the colour of moonlight. "Sophie Smith belongs here too!" he cried, and his voice echoed in the emptiness overhead.

"Don't be so loud." The echo made her tremble.

"There's no one here, Sophie. We're alone."

"I thought I heard something." A curving staircase seemed supported on nothing but shadow, and she had the wild notion that something moved there.

"There's a ghost," he said.

She tried to make light of it. "I thought there would be," she said, but he seemed not to hear.

"My mother polishes that staircase," he said. "She hoovers the carpet, then polishes the handrail. Room by room she goes through this house. She should know all about the ghost."

He paused, and Sophie said, "Does she?"

"Does she what?" He was haughty.

"Does she know about the ghost?"

"Of course."

"Has she told you?"

"She doesn't have to mention it." He spoke as if the question was hardly worth answering. "You know it was in this house that he died."

She did know, but she had to distance herself from it. She found herself saying, "I thought it happened abroad."

"Oh no. Clive Millwood hanged himself here. I can take you to the room." He headed towards the foot of the stairs, but Sophie hung back. "What's wrong?" he wanted to know.

"I'm cold."

"You're not afraid, are you?"

"I'm cold!" Anger made her turn to the open door and step outside. She began to run and had reached the foot of the steps before he caught up with her.

"Sophie." He held her close. "I'm sorry." He kissed her. "I shouldn't be like that; not with you." He tried to say more but she put her lips against his and prevented his words.

Together they walked away from the house towards the rose garden. "You are," he said, "you really are."

"What am I?"

"The prettiest girl ever. I love you, Sophie."

The roses had lost all their colour. They were black in the moonlight, more beautiful than by day.

"Sophie," he murmured. "I don't want you to go."

"I know."

"So stay with me. Stay the night."

"How can I, Martin?"

"If we went to the Hall no one would find us." He had every detail worked out. She could, he told her, get away from her home in the village after everyone had gone to bed. He would meet her at the Hall, "and if anyone finds out we can say we've been ghost hunting."

"I can't," she said. "You know I can't."

He drew back and mimicked her, putting a cruel whine into his voice: "I can't, I can't. My mother will find out and I shall be in trouble."

But it was not fear of trouble that held her back. She did not care how much trouble she went through for him; it was love that prevented her staying with him. Love was a bargain that was not sealed with acts of love; it was a fierce balance, a savage tenderness that stripped off more than clothes. Keeping apart was sometimes part of love.

"Martin," she said. Behind him the moon disturbed the topmost leaves of the trees like a carp pushing its silver belly through weed. "I love you, Martin."

"But not enough to be with me." He turned away and looked towards the Hall. The rows of windows cut the moonlight into black squares. "All those rooms are just for us," he said. "We could dance in the ballroom, climb the stairs by moonlight, go where we pleased, and no one would know."

A great tiredness swept over her. "I'm too afraid, Martin," she said. It was not the truth; the truth was that she loved him too much for everything to depend on what she did or did not do in a single night. He was putting her to the test, and the test was false. She was so tired she began to weep.

"The moon will go to waste," he said. "It will never be like this again."

"I know." She sat where she was, her head bowed, with all the prettiness his mother had praised washed away by weeping.

"So will you do it?"

He stood in front of her, looking down. She ached to be with him, but she shook her head.

The night held its breath, and then his feet stirred the gravel. She was suddenly happy. She knew that gentleness had overcome him and he was stooping towards her. She raised her head, smiling.

But she was mistaken. He had turned his back on her and was already walking away.

He left the path and his footfalls were silent on

the lawn. The big house that could have been theirs, where they could have whispered together all through the night, lay in front of him. She saw him as he climbed the steps, then lost sight of him in the shadows of the portico.

It was still not too late. Sophie thought she saw him standing between the columns, waiting for her, and she started to her feet.

Martin knew she would change her mind. She was too perfect, too desirable to deny what the moon was doing for them in the night. She would come to meet him.

They gazed towards each other through the moonlight until the shape she thought was Martin dissolved. And then, as faintly as a distant householder locking up for the night, the sound of a door closing reached her from beyond the lawn.

The house, like a vast, motionless heart, lay all around him. "And it's yours, Sophie," he murmured, "if you cared to take it."

Sophie, beginning to turn away, put out a hand and touched a rose.

Moonlight, filtering into the well of the hall, showed the great sweep of the staircase curving down like a dragon's tongue to the marble floor, and Martin looked up. Often, standing there, he had heard the sound of his mother's vacuum cleaner swallowed and made insignificant as she went about her rounds, but now the small sound of his own breathing spread outwards to fill all the space. Sophie's breath could have mingled with his.

"Hell!" he said aloud. "Hell!"

He began to climb the stairs, running his hand

along the banister that his mother had to dust while Joe Medlicott was outside mowing the lawns.

"Nothing is right!" he cried up into the darkness. "Everything is wrong!"

He climbed the stairs to the broad landing. The sheeted furniture was spaced around him like dim icebergs, and he moved between them to look over the balustrade. Sophie had cheated him. They should be moving together now, exploring mysteries.

Anger made him beat the rail. "And the ghost!" he shouted. "We would have found the ghost!"

He fell silent. Clive Millwood had died up here. And Martin knew where. He had found out long ago even though nobody had wanted to tell him. It was a secret he carried with him, and Sophie could have shared it.

"But she didn't dare!"

Sophie had the rose in her fingers. Its petals were too tender. She crushed it, and her hand closed on a thorn.

Martin struck the banister again. Only an intolerable weakness would send him down the stairs and out into the moonlit parkland. He had to continue alone.

He hesitated. The door of the corner stairs to the top floor was almost hidden, as if it did not want to be seen. There was time yet to turn back.

Sophie pressed on the thorn until she felt blood on her fingers.

Martin turned the door handle and went through. The staircase was no wider than a cupboard and was boarded on both sides. He felt his way upwards until, bumping against the upper door in the blackness, he made the latch rattle. It startled him, and he realized he had been climbing silently as if he were afraid of disturbing someone. But the house was empty. He himself was the only patch of warmth and movement in all its passages and hollow rooms.

Sophie opened her hand and saw the darkness of the blood in her palm.

Martin pushed the door. It opened into a corridor under the roof. Curtainless windows stretched away in a long line on one side, and dark doorways on the other. Servants had once lived here, a small township of them, always busy, and at any time a door had been likely to open. But now only his own presence disturbed the dust.

He stepped into the corridor, leaving the stairway door open behind him. The room he sought was at the far end, beyond the slant of faint moonlight through the furthermost window.

He moved two slow paces, and a third. He took a fourth step, then stood still. Uncertainty crept into him, and he looked back. Sophie should have been with him. By mocking her fear he would have overcome his own.

Sophie bowed her head over her hand, and the smart of the thorn brought tears to her eyes.

The heat of the summer day still lingered under the roof, but Martin's skin was cold. The stairs he had just climbed had long been unused; now one of them, settling back, cracked. He ceased to breathe.

From the black opening of the staircase the faintest of shuffling sounds came whispering towards him. A moth must have been trapped and was beating its dusty wings in a blind corner. Or it was a secret footfall.

He stumbled and the sudden thud of his heel drummed in the space behind him and sent him running away from the stairhead. The floorboards were barred with moonlight like rafters over emptiness, and the air pushed at his face and attempted to hold him back. But the slowness was an illusion. He ran full tilt into the door at the corridor's end and it burst open.

Sophie looked towards the house, but it was blurred by the moisture in her eyes.

Martin staggered into the room, twisted and looked back. The stairhead at the far end of the corridor gaped wider. He was sure of it. He slammed the door shut, felt a key under his fingers and turned it. The lock shot to, but the key fell to the floor.

He heard it clatter on the boards and stooped to find it. A single window, high up, let down a faded light that showed a chair beside a bed, and on the bed a rolled mattress. The key was invisible. He sank to his knees, sweeping the boards with his fingers.

The night was silent. Sophie let her tears fall.

No sound came from the corridor. Martin knew it was empty, peopled only by panic. Clive Millwood had died in this room, but there was no ghost. He refused to allow a ghost. His fingertip touched the cold metal of the key and he let his head sag with relief.

Sophie got to her feet just as Martin's fingernail nudged the key a fraction. It tilted into a crack between the boards and fell away. A flick and gone.

Sophie began to walk away.

Still kneeling, Martin raised his head. On the bed, a figure was crouching like himself. No, it was only the rolled mattress. He gazed at it, and it began to crawl towards the foot of the bed.

Sophie dried her eyes and licked the blood from her palm.

Martin crabbed backwards along the boards as the figure swung its legs to the floor and stood upright. He pushed back further, but the door stopped him. The hollow eyes in the narrow face were full of sorrow as the figure came shuffling forward until it stood over him. Its long arms reached down to him.

Sophie, in the long avenue, heading homeward, heard a scream. She thought it was an owl.

EELS

Rosemary was ten when she was smothered by Aunt Jenny and fed to the eels.

Oh, dear me, how easy it was. Poor lamb, to go so sweetly. But I was very angry at the time. "And the strange thing is," said Miss Jenny Jervis aloud, "I am a single lady without brothers or sisters, so I'm not really her aunt."

"Everyone knows that," said Mrs Berry. "When's that blasted bus coming?" They were waiting at Church Bridge for the bingo bus to take them to Terrington out across the fens.

"But she always calls me auntie – I can't think why."

"And I can't think why you suddenly started to come to bingo. Gambling – that ain't like you, Jenny Jervis."

Miss Jervis simpered. "Maybe I'm feeling lucky, Phoebe." *Heavens, yes. Very lucky. First Rosemary with the eels, and now Rosemary's mother has passed away. By accident. So she'll never come looking for her darling little Rosemary again. How very convenient. No need of eels for her.* "I feel fresh as a daisy today," said Miss Jervis. "Free as a bird."

"Damned if you don't look it." Mrs Berry cast an eye over the flowered dress, the gloves and the

75

white hat with a hint of veil across Miss Jervis's brow. "It's not a wedding, you know – only bloody bingo."

"It pleases you to be blunt, Phoebe," said Miss Jervis, "but other people are not so unkind. Rosemary for one – although," she added modestly, "I still can't think why she has always been so nice to me."

"Don't come that with me," said Mrs Berry. "You know well enough." The bus came drifting along the waterside. "And for God's sake help me up these blasted steps."

Mrs Berry, unlike Miss Jervis, was fat and her hips were so bad she could hardly lift her feet. She handed over her stick before she grasped the handrail. "And wipe that stupid expression off of your face, Jenny Jervis. The girl calls you auntie because she loves you, God knows why."

Miss Jervis held the stick by the middle and kept it clear of the ground in case germs ran up it and into her gloves. "I've only been doing my duty by the girl," she said.

"Duty be blowed." Mrs Berry's grunt was muffled in her fat bosom as she heaved her way upwards. "Who cares about duty? – you don't, for one."

"You are wrong there, Phoebe." Miss Jervis regarded the broad rear end. *Quite wrong. My duty was to despatch the child. She should never have been born, so it was her destiny, the darling.* "I have a strong sense of duty," she said.

"Squit! You have a strong sense of looking after number one – like the rest of us."

"Here's your stick, dear." Miss Jervis handed it over, and dusted off the tips of her gloves.

"And don't call me dear!" Mrs Berry had found a seat and was peeling the wrapper from a pack of king size. "I'm not in a bloody rest home yet."

The bus began to move, and Miss Jervis looked down into the river as it slid by. *Silly to call it a river, but they all do. It's a drainage cut, as they very well know, because the water's quite still and not like a river at all. Fortunate, really, because I knew just where Rosemary was until the eels had finished with her. It was quite hygienic. All I had to do was wrap up the bones and put them in the dustbin a few at a time until there was nothing left. Nothing.*

"What you smiling at?"

"Just thoughts," said Miss Jervis.

"Once a school teacher, always a bloody school teacher. You're just the same as you was when you was a kid, Jenny Jervis. Anyone could've seen you was never really going to put that school behind you."

"Don't get so cross with me, Phoebe. There's nothing wrong with being a teacher." *Headmistress, actually, when I retired. And what did you ever do, fat Phoebe?* "I love being with children," she said.

"You never showed much sign of it." Mrs Berry plugged a cigarette into her plump face and waved a flame at it. "You never got married, did you? Never had no children of your own, never hardly got away from this village where you was born."

"I was away at training college for three years, don't forget."

"Training college." Mrs Berry clicked her tongue. "That must've been a riot."

Phoebe, Phoebe, I had a baby. The rhyme sprang to Miss Jervis's mind and made her smile. *I had a baby, and I don't mean maybe.* She looked out of the window.

Mrs Berry, who had been watching her from the corner of her eye, said, "You can't tell me you girls didn't get up to some fun and games when you was away from home."

Miss Jervis raised her eyebrows. "We were training to be *teachers*, Phoebe, so nothing very terrible happened." *Except, of course, I had a baby girl and couldn't come home for a while.* "And anyway," she smiled, "even if there had been something I was ashamed of I wouldn't have let anyone know, would I?"

"You're grinning like a cat what's had the cream," said Mrs Berry.

"Am I? I wonder why." *And you may well turn away with that disgusted expression on your face, fat Phoebe, because now there's no chance at all you'll ever find out anything.* Using both hands, Miss Jervis smoothed her dress firmly across her thighs and spoke to herself very clearly: *And wouldn't you just love to know that the daughter I had was adopted and grew up to have a daughter of her own? And that little girl was Rosemary — so I'm not her auntie; I'm her granny. I'm a granny, Phoebe, just like you.* "Anyway," she said mischievously, "I don't suppose my sins will ever come home to roost now."

"Not that you ever had none."

"Not that I ever had any," said Miss Jervis primly, but she could not help a shiver, because her sin very nearly had come home to roost. Not long since. *But you don't know that, Phoebe. I had my baby adopted the day after she was born and I thought she was gone for ever.* Miss Jervis closed her eyes. *And then ... after all those years ... she found me!* "It was a terrible moment" – the words came out before she could stop them.

"What was?"

"I mean it must be a terrible moment when your sins catch up with you." She gave a little grimace. *You'll never catch me out, Phoebe fatbum. Not now. Rosemary has gone, and now my dear daughter is also no longer with us.* "Did you read about that awful plane crash?" she asked.

"What about it?" Mrs Berry was annoyed at the sudden change of subject.

"Well, I was just wondering about those poor people. Their sins caught up with them, didn't they?" *My daughter, for one. She dumped that Rosemary on me, and threatened to give away my secret if I didn't take her, just so she could gad about with her boyfriend. Well, now she's gone, her and her boyfriend. Serve 'em both right.* Miss Jervis had read the passenger list. "It's so sad," she said.

"Not that you look it."

"Well, it's such a lovely day." *And I'm so lucky. Nobody left to ask questions about Rosemary; no more blackmail from Rosemary's mother.*

"I can't never fathom you out." Mrs Berry, because her fat legs pressed into the seat in front, let

79

ash dribble into her lap. "You was headmistress, with your own little house by the river, everything you ever wanted – and then you had to go and saddle yourself with that kid Rosemary. At your time of life."

"It was because of a friend from the old days." *A friend! I mean my dear daughter – happily no longer with us.* "And my little home was just perfect for the two of us."

"Well, kids are kids – I wonder you could stand having your place messed up."

"But it was no problem, Phoebe, no problem at all." *Until the stupid child began to whine for the mother who didn't want her.* "Because she is such a sweet little girl," said Miss Jervis. *Was a little girl. And sweet at the end. She drifted away so softly under her pillow she could hardly have felt its touch.* "So sweet," sighed Miss Jervis.

"Sweet as a sugar plum, no doubt, but it was never your way to burden yourself."

"You have a cruel tongue, Phoebe, but my deeds speak louder than words."

"Hark at little Miss Prim. Never done a thing wrong in her whole life – I *don't* think."

It was said so knowingly that Miss Jervis felt a touch of anxiety. "I don't understand you," she said.

"I know something you done, Jenny Jervis ... something you was ashamed of."

Mrs Berry's eyes suddenly had such a hard glint that Miss Jervis looked away. *But it couldn't be Rosemary. Everybody believed me when I said she'd gone home to her mother.*

"You was a naughty girl once." Mrs Berry was sly, and waited to see the effect. "That's made you go pale, ain't it?"

"There's nothing on my conscience, Phoebe."

"Well, there should be."

Miss Jervis sat quite still.

"You gone white just like you did then. First you went white, then you went red and then you started to cry and said it wasn't your fault. You'd have done anything to stop other people knowing what you done. And I was the one who could've shamed you, Jenny Jervis."

Miss Jervis made a tiny movement with her gloves.

"I see you remember it now – that day when we was kids and you snitched some sweets from a girl's desk." Her eyes were on Miss Jervis. "And I seen you do it."

"Is that all?" Miss Jervis let out her breath.

"*All*, you say. *All*."

"I was only trying to put her books straight." Miss Jervis was annoyed to find that her mouth had gone dry.

"Then why did you snivel and grovel and promise me anything so long as I wouldn't tell? Books my foot!"

"But..."

"No buts. You're still making excuses. You never did give a thought to that poor girl you was thieving from – all you cared about was that you shouldn't be shamed. That's what you was afraid of – shame."

Miss Jervis took a handkerchief from her glove.

"I think you're trying to spoil my little outing, Phoebe."

"And now it's tears. Just as it always was. You haven't changed one little bit."

Miss Jervis blew her nose. "I'm relieved that I haven't any worse skeletons in my cupboard," she said. "Perhaps I'm lucky."

And she was. She won at bingo. She could do nothing wrong, and knew it in her bones. So when the old woman sitting next to her was careless with her purse, Miss Jervis dipped her fingers into it and came out with a note.

She was putting it into her handbag before she realized she had been spotted. A finger was pointed, and silence spread outwards from where she sat until the hall was full of waxworks with every head turned her way.

"But I was only helping her to buy her tickets," she said, and the silence deepened.

Outside, Mrs Berry said, "Get on the bus and shut up." She made Miss Jervis sit next to the window and sat beside her to wedge her in and prevent her getting to the aisle. "I don't want you flinging yourself off of this bus and making more trouble for everybody."

Miss Jervis's voice had almost gone. "I was only going to give her some change for her tickets," she whispered. Her throat hurt.

"Just stay quiet." Mrs Berry was smoking hard. "Nobody wants to hear you."

There had been a lot of chatter and laughter on the bus going out. Now the sound of voices barely rose above the rumble of the wheels, and all the women watched in silence when it drew up at the waterside and Mrs Berry and Miss Jervis got off.

"You look a bit tottery." Mrs Berry, leaning on her stick, took pity on her. "Would you like to have a cup of tea with me?"

"No thank you, Phoebe."

It was dusk, but the air was still warm. Mrs Berry tried to make conversation. "Lovely evening," she said. "Lot of midges, though." They could just be seen above the pale surface of the water, dancing in congregations. Before long they would be invisible. Miss Jervis watched them but said nothing.

"Don't worry about it," said Mrs Berry. "It won't seem so bad in the morning." She breathed heavily, as though kindliness cost her an effort. "None of us is perfect."

Miss Jervis murmured good night, and Mrs Berry watched until she had trailed slowly across the road to her front door, fumbled for her key and let herself in.

Mrs Berry walked painfully away. "Stupid bloody woman," she grunted. "Looks as if she wants to do away with herself. Well, she shouldn't have done what she done in the first place."

Miss Jervis did, in fact, have death in mind. How could she face anyone ever again? She put on her nightdress but did not go to bed. Instead she sat by the empty fireplace until the daylight had washed itself out of the sky, and then she opened her front door and went barefoot across the road to the waterside. She had unpinned her hair, and the grey strands hung loosely. It no longer mattered.

She went carefully, out of habit, down the grassy bank, and before her toes touched the water she leant over and looked down. The movement allowed her unpinned hair to brush her face, and saved her life.

The touch of her hair swinging against her face made her automatically lift her head to brush it away, and it was then she saw the midges. Phoebe Berry was right; there were clouds of them. As they gyrated they made shapes as wispy as bubbles on the point of bursting. If creatures so flimsy continued to exist, why should she die?

Miss Jervis turned away, and slipped. She should have known how treacherous the bank was because it was here she had weighted Rosemary for the eels. But now she had let both feet slide into the water, and she had to struggle before she managed to get a tight enough grip on the grass to crawl up the bank.

The edge of her nightgown was wet and clung to her ankles as she crossed the road, and as soon as she was indoors she changed it.

"Now a nice hot cup of tea, Miss Jervis," she said, lecturing herself, "and no more nonsense."

The sound of her own voice made her feel stronger. She would go to bingo again and brazen it out. She would be generous, so generous that they would all be overwhelmed with guilt for accusing her. And then *she* would forgive *them*, and they would respect her even more.

"Because you stand for something in this village," she told herself, "and always will." She dried her feet vigorously. "Now off to bed with you."

84

Despite the rubbing, her feet and ankles remained cold so she took a hot water bottle with her. The bed was soon luxuriously warm, and her mind was at rest.

She slept so soundly that she awoke with cramp down one side and nothing would ease the pain until she moved about her room. It was still dark, and she pulled aside the curtains, as she had so often done, to look at the water and be certain that nothing was disturbing Rosemary. That worry was done with for ever.

It was a summer's night and enough light filtered from the sky to show the smooth face of the river, and even the track of bent grass she had left in the verge. And her wet footprints still led to the door.

"The sun will be my friend," she said. "All will be dry soon."

She slid back into bed. The water bottle was cold and she pushed it to one side, but its coolness lingered. She thrust it further away and gasped with annoyance. It must have burst because a cold wetness was on her feet. She sat up and reached down. The chill rubber was clammy. Slimy. It slipped under her fingers as though it was moving. She flung it out of bed. It slapped the floor, but she had used too much violence because she heard it slither further.

"Damn!" Miss Jervis never swore, but she was angry. The water bottle would be leaking all over the floor, and she also had to change the bed. "Damn!"

She threw aside the bedcover, but the damp sheet had twisted around her feet. She was reaching

85

down to untangle herself when her heart thudded. She was not alone in the room. Silhouetted against the window was a shape.

Fear had made Miss Jervis cringe backwards, but suddenly she leant forward, and now her heart was pounding with anger. The silhouette was human. But it was neither tall nor broad. It was a child. One of her pupils. Some stupid prank.

"Get out!" It was a classroom order. "Get out at once!"

The child, however, came forward, slowly and heavily. Its footsteps dragged as if with a great weight.

"I'll see you pay for this!"

Miss Jervis gathered herself to lunge, but her feet would not obey her. They would not move. She reached down. The bed was wet and cold, but it was not the sheet that had trapped her feet. Something slippery had coiled itself around her ankles. And it was moving. She felt something slide between her toes and tenderly begin to stroke her leg.

"No!" she cried. "No!"

Feverishly, trying to pull back at the same time, she reached down. Her fingers plunged into a nest of eels.

Miss Jervis screamed. She flung her hands to the bedrail to haul herself free. She struggled. The cold grip tightened and held her legs still. She could not move.

She was whimpering as the child came closer. Its footsteps slithered and squelched and it brought the darkness of deep water into the room. It stopped by the bedside, and a hand reached out to hold hers. If it was a hand. Miss Jervis never knew.

The child's fingers writhed and were slimy. And the child's head, when it bent over her, had many damp tendrils of hair that, eager and slippery, reached out to busily caress her face, loving her.

When the sun came up and filled the room with warmth, Miss Jervis lay quite still. Her nightgown, however, heaved with a life of its own.

DEATH WISH

Dawn barely showed above the rim of darkness when Emma Boyce stepped into the lane and began her long walk home. She had no coat and the thin material covering her shoulders was punctured by a shower of droplets from a tree. Even though she shivered she did not notice she was cold.

There had been talk of murder. Two days ago, Emma had been sitting in the common room, stroking the cat and listening. She had not realized that she was being watched.

"Why is it so often a girl who gets killed?" said one of the girls. "What's wrong with giving a boy the chop once in a while?"

There was a laugh, then another girl, prettier and aware of it, said, "You take a chance when you're out with a boy." There were some shrieks of protest, but she persisted. "Well, I do. There's always a risk."

"You love it."

She tried to quiet the laughter. "Be serious. I think girls are a kind of temptation to them just because they are bigger and stronger ... the boys, I mean." She was giggling. "Anyway that's what I like about them ... mostly. So it's just a risk we've got to take, in my opinion."

There were cries of "No!" from both sexes.

"I don't feel..." one of the boys began.

"Oh, yes you do, Philip!" said the girl with the good looks, and she got a cheer.

"I don't feel it's right," he insisted, "to be talking about killing like this. We're making it sound as if death had something to do with sex."

It was then that Emma raised her eyes from the cat and saw that she was being watched. Simon Ewart was gazing at her. It had never happened before; not like that, not so intently. She was not pretty enough to draw that kind of look from someone like him, and suddenly, angrily, she cried aloud, "It's not fair!"

The room went silent. The stupidity of what she had done made her dig her fingers into the cat's back. Instead of spitting at her it stretched in an ecstasy and suddenly, as if she had picked up its electricity, she knew what to say.

"It's not fair to blame people. They don't mean to kill each other – not if they're in love. It's just that love and death seem to go hand in hand sometimes. I mean..." And, as suddenly as it had arisen, inspiration left her. She did not know what she meant. She dipped her head.

One of the boys sighed and said to a friend, "What's got into her?"

"She's got the hots for someone, I reckon. Look how she's stroking that lucky cat."

And then, because they could see she was embarrassed, they talked about other things. She hated herself. She would never have needed their kindness, their condescension, if her nose had been straighter. And Simon Ewart was worse than the rest. He had gazed at her as if she, like he himself, belonged in the ranks of the handsome and the beautiful. He had made her cry out and betray herself.

The common room emptied, but she remained where she was, engrossed in the cat. It was not until she looked up that she saw that Simon Ewart had also stayed behind. He even held out a hand to help her to her feet and she let the cat slide from her lap and stood up. She knew it was farcical. Boy meets girl. What came next? A date? Perhaps it's the cat, she thought. He likes the way I stroked it.

"Oh, well," she said, "I don't mind."

"Sorry?" Dark eyes, black eyebrows and olive skin; he was so handsome she wanted to laugh.

She spoke lightly. "I don't mind going out with you, Simon."

"How on earth did you know I was going to ask?"

Surprise struck so hard that her hand, as if she truly were in a story, flew to her heart. Then she recovered. "Can this," she said, "be the start of a teenage romance?"

"That's up to you, Emma."

She noted the blush that darkened his already dark cheeks, and her heart began to pound in earnest.

"Damn!" she said and closed her eyes. "Damn, damn and double-damn!"

He did not understand, and said so.

"I can't believe I'm saying this," she did not look at him, "but why me?"

"And I might just as well say, why me?"

For the first time she realized that they were still holding hands. It was so laughably stupid she wanted to cry.

"I wasn't going to come straight out with it," he said, "but you've forced me. You're not the same as the rest."

Not as pretty. She risked a quick look up at him, then dropped her eyes. "How do you mean?"

"It was something you said about people in love."

She freed her fingers from his. "I said they killed each other. That's what I said."

"So they do." He waited until her eyes met his. "In a way. They lose themselves. They cease to be what they were. That's dying." When she made no reply, he said, "You said so yourself, but nobody else thought it worth bothering about. They just dropped it."

"I don't blame them. It's rubbish." Her scorn was running away with her. She was hurting herself, deliberately, and she did not know why. Giddiness almost made her cling to his arm. She longed to touch him, and he would have welcomed it. Instead, she found herself saying, "Nobody dies for love."

He was silent. Now she knew she had succeeded in driving him away. The floor interested her as she waited to be dismissed. But his words, when they came, were a puzzle.

"Oh yes, they do," he said.

"Who do? Do what?"

"People. They die for love."

Was that all? She sighed and looked away.

"Stop trying to push me aside, Emma."

"Am I?" She forced herself to be languid.

"You seem to be." He spoke so intensely that she tried, absurdly, to stare him down. She failed. "People do die for love, Emma."

"Do they?" She heard the meekness in her voice before she knew that the edge had left it. "I've never heard of it."

"But I have. They do die and I can prove it."

"I expect you can." It was little more than a whisper; from disdain she had plunged headlong into surrender.

"I'll show you a place where it happened," he said.

It was a hot afternoon when he borrowed his father's car and took her out of the city to the church on the hill. The village to which the church belonged had long since disappeared, and the church stood alone under the sun except that, between the graveyard yews, they could see the rector's house. "He has two other churches," Simon told her, "so we may not see him."

The shimmer of heat over the sloping fields bred a silence that lay like sleep in the churchyard. "It's hard to believe," he said, "but this was where it happened, long ago."

"It's so quiet I can hardly breathe," said Emma.

"That's why they chose it, I expect. It was a good place for lovers." He led her along the narrow path to the base of the church tower. "And one of them is still here."

They stood by the gravestone. It read: *Amy Burgess 1960–1977*.

"That's not so long ago," said Emma. "And you didn't tell me she was so young." Seventeen. A year older than herself.

"They found her in the corner over there." He pointed to where the flint wall of the churchyard vanished into a bramble thicket. "Her family cut a cross in the turf where her body lay."

"You'd think they'd want to forget."

"Well, they've moved away since then, and it's been neglected. But you can still see it."

They went through the long grass together and stood at the edge of the bramble clump. In spite of the heat Emma shuddered and he said, "You've only yourself to blame. You shouldn't have been so interested in murder."

"But I'm not – not a bit." Her doubts about being with him had returned. The dress she wore was too attractive; it was too ambitious for her looks, and soon he would notice. "I hate murder," she said. "Hate it."

"If that's the truth, Emma," he said mildly, "why are you here?"

"I don't know. Because you asked me, I suppose," and then, before he could reply, she turned back to the brambles. "It's dark in there." The sunlight was absorbed long before it reached the heart of the clump. "I can't see a thing."

He pressed down the edge of the thorns with his foot and leant over the tangle. "But it's still there." He straightened and stamped again at the brambles to help her penetrate the thicket. Still she could see nothing.

"And I can't move," she said. "I'm trapped."

"Just like poor Amy Burgess," he stood alongside her, "on that dark night fourteen years ago."

"When I was two." All she could see was stale earth within the bank of thorns, but a girl had died there. Tears suddenly stung her eyes. Love never came out right. "How did she die?" She did not take her eyes from the darkness.

"She was strangled. Her lover strangled her."

"But why, if he loved her?"

"Who knows?"

"And then they caught him?"

"They didn't have to. They found him next morning a long way from here. Hanging in a railway carriage."

They had died the same night, but miles apart. A tear escaped at last and ran down Emma's cheek.

"It's just as you said, Emma. Love and death go hand in hand."

It was true. She knew it. There was always something that had to die. "I still can't see the cross," she said.

"The trouble is, Emma, if I'm going to help you I shall have to hold you."

She remained still, saying nothing. Even that was an invitation, and shyness made her glance quickly over her shoulder.

"Hell, Emma," he said, "but you are pretty!"

No, I'm not. His dark eyes outshone her own. He was the beautiful one. "It's hot," she said. The whole churchyard sang with grasshoppers, and she wanted to tune her voice to them and whisper words she dared not form in her mind. What her lips said was, "The sun is burning."

"And you want to see the cross." Nothing more about her looks. He cleared more space so that she could step deeper into the brambles and he stood behind her. "Be careful you don't fall." He put his arm around her waist and she leant forward, letting him take her weight.

"Your belly shrinks away under my hand," he said.

"I can't help it."

"You are so soft."

"Because..." and then she dared not go on. "You shouldn't say belly," she said, and he laughed. She gazed deeper into the brambles. "I think I can see something. A sort of trough, a little ditch."

"That's all that's left. It's where she died."

Once again sadness swept through her.

"You're trembling, Emma."

She moved as if she were making an effort to escape, but all she achieved was to turn within his arm. He kissed her, but she clenched her hands together under her chin and did not respond.

"You're not afraid of me, are you, Emma?"

"No." She tilted her face away from him. "Yes."

"I'd never hurt you."

"I know."

"But you are afraid. It's not because of what happened here, is it?"

She pressed her knuckles into her mouth. "I don't know." But she did know. There were worse ways of being hurt than being killed. His handsome face hurt her. She did not have beauty enough to match him. She could never hold him. Nothing was more certain.

"And now you are crying." He spoke so softly his words were dissolved in the heat. "You are crying for Amy Burgess."

"No." A wren flickered suddenly through the brambles and she reached up and pulled his face close to hers. "I'm crying because of me – that's what's making me cry. Because of me – because of you." They kissed so fiercely she could not breathe and when, eventually, he tried to speak she put her hand over his mouth.

"Don't ask me anything," she said. "I know a girl was strangled just here, but I don't care." The whole of life was rolled up in death, so what did it matter? "I don't care!"

Clumsily, half falling, they stepped clear of the brambles, and she was dragging him down into the long grass when his arm tightened around her waist and held her upright. He was looking beyond her.

"What is it?" She twisted and saw that a figure was wending its way towards them through the rectory garden.

Simon straightened, easing himself away from her. "It's my heavenly father," he said.

"But you told me the rector was away somewhere."

He saw her smoothing her dress. "You're not nervous, are you?"

"No," she lied.

"I'd better warn you," he said, "the Dad's hot on sex."

"For or against?" She heard him laugh, but panic swept over her. She had known, everybody knew, his father was a parson. But this one! How could she have been so stupid as not to guess? Her hand flew to her mouth. "Oh, God!"

"No – he's still only the rector."

A pale egg of a bald head on a thin, black-clad body came through the gap where a rusty gate was jammed permanently open, and Simon stepped forward.

"Emma, this is my father," he said. "Father, this is the girl I didn't tell you about."

The rector's face was scored by deep lines like the long footprint of a heron. He held out a thin hand.

"I'm pleased to meet you," she said, and heard herself add, out of cowardice, "sir."

At that he raised his eyebrows, and the long lines of his face shed their harshness. He was amused. "And I am pleased to meet you, ma'am."

He mimicked her politeness and made her blush, but his smile was kind. He was not the bloodless cleric he appeared to be. Even his hand was warm. "I imagine my son has been giving you a conducted tour of the morbid pleasures of the churchyard," he said.

"Emma is interested in murder," said Simon. "That's why we're here."

The rector preferred to talk of other matters. "Emma," he said. "Allow me to be parsonical, and say that that is a pretty name. I hope you will stay to tea, Emma."

Simon's comment had been brushed aside and he did not like it. "She wanted to see where Amy Burgess was killed." His already dark face darkened still further. "I was showing her where the body was found, Father."

"Yes. Quite so." The rector agreed too hastily, as if he stood in awe of his son and was afraid to confront him. Instead, he glanced shyly at Emma and said, "Don't be carried away, my dear. Terrible deeds can have too great a hold on some imaginations." And then, as if unwilling to take part in any argument, he turned and began to walk back to the house.

"Some imaginations!" Simon's anger flared as the narrow shoulders retreated. "He's just what he looks like – a condescending old bigot!"

"But nice with it." Emma saw a lonely old man walking through an overgrown garden and felt sorry for him.

"Nice? I'll show you how nice he is!" Simon turned and she had no choice but to go with him towards the church.

Inside, insulated from the sun by its thick walls of flint, the church was a huge fistful of coldness. Simon, familiar with it, seemed not to notice, and in the vestry he was unaffected by the dejected row of surplices hanging limply against the wall or the gritty piles of damp hymn books. He found a key to unlock a door in a pointed arch, and as it swung back a slow turbulence of even colder air slid around them.

"A good place to bring a book," he said, and she followed him up a narrow spiral stair.

They came out into a room with a high ceiling, and he noticed she was hugging herself against the chill.

"I sit on that ledge." He pointed to where a single wedge of dusty sunlight came through a high window. "It's warm there."

"And quiet," Emma said. The damp smell of whitewash deadened all sound.

"It used to be noisy. Until the Dad got busy, that is. I'll show you."

He led her into an even narrower stairway, so steep that as they climbed his feet were level with her head, and they emerged into a room of such stony dimness that she could barely see the walls.

"The hanging chamber," he said. "That's its name."

They stood on the edge of a square pit in the floor. Thick beams, like the crosspieces of gallows, spanned the gap and beneath them dim shapes like grey, hunched shoulders hung in the blackness.

Emma saw hanged men. "They're dead!" Her voice was a moan that was swallowed by the pit.

"Dead as doornails."

Simon was unconcerned and she was about to twist towards him when she saw that her eyes had deceived her. The grey shoulders belonged to bells, not men. "I feel so stupid. I thought they were..." She could not bring herself to say it. Instead, she said, "That's what you meant by noise. The bells."

"Oh, those." He seemed not to have noticed them. "They haven't been rung for years."

"But you said..."

"It wasn't bells that made all the din – it was them." She turned with him, putting the pit filled with crouching bells behind her, and looked where he was pointing.

There was a single window opening in the wall, but it was blocked by the overlapping slats of a louvre and a heavy wire mesh. Just enough light filtered through to show a row of small, rounded shapes on the sill. "They made a great racket," he said, "until the Dad put a stop to them."

She leant forward, but drew back quickly. "Pigeons," she said. "They're dead."

"Of course they are." He reached to pick one up, but she held him back.

"But how?"

"Well, you'd be dead if you were shut up without any food." He pointed to where a part of the rusty wire mesh had been covered by a piece of board. "There used to be a hole in that corner. It was blocked off."

"With the pigeons still inside?" She saw him nod. "But surely not by your father. He's not like that."

"No?" He crouched and put a hand out to one of the birds. "Lovely creatures," he said. "You wouldn't think they'd been dead for years, would you?"

She shook her head.

"But they have. It happened when I was little, just after my mother died. I used to come up here a lot, and I found them and put them in a row. They're only skin and bone, you know. And feathers." He stroked one with the back of his hand.

"I couldn't do that. I can't even bear to watch." Emma retreated, and he went with her.

Outside, a breeze had sprung up and the grass was bending. "Don't let my father frighten you," he said, "but whatever you do don't mention the pigeons."

"I won't."

The promise, however, hardly seemed to be needed because it was Simon himself who, throughout teatime, seemed to be continually skirting the subject.

"Emma likes your church, Father," he said. "She wanted to see it all – the belfry, everything."

"Ah, the bells." The rector shook his head. "They have been silent ever since they have been in my charge. A sad place, I'm afraid."

"Very sad." Simon, looking down at his plate, paused, then said, "I even took her up to the hanging chamber."

"But that's unsafe!" The rector was alarmed.

"Emma knows that well enough, Father. I believe she thought she was seeing ghosts up there."

"I didn't say that." Emma looked quickly from one to the other. "It was the bells. At first sight they looked like men hanging there. But I didn't say anything, I know I didn't."

"You didn't have to," said Simon, "and it wasn't the bells I meant."

There was a gap of silence, and then his father changed the subject. "I do believe we ought to have had tea in the kitchen as usual." He sat back and moved his head to take in the long dining room. "It's far cosier than this gloomy barrack."

The tea cloth took up only one end of the huge table, a patch of brightness surrounded by dark furniture. The rector smiled at Emma. "There's so much space," he said, "that we may as well be outside having a picnic."

"Except for the weather." She looked towards the window where a flurry of rain rattled the pane. "Listen to that."

"It's ghostly pigeons," said Simon, "tapping on the pane because they don't like the cold and dark." He stood up. "Should I let them in, Father?"

The rector waved a hand asking him to sit down. "Don't frighten the young lady, there's a good chap."

"But there *are* ghosts around this house, Emma, and not only pigeons. Did you know that something else was starved to death?"

"Take it easy, dear boy." The rector was smoothing the table cloth nervously. "You know the cat was an accident."

"And the pigeons in the tower?"

"I know nothing about pigeons, Simon. You're the only one who ever goes up there." He turned to Emma, shamefaced. "I'm afraid of heights. Simon's the brave one. And the cat was no one's fault. When Simon was a little boy..." – he patted the air to prevent his son interrupting – "some workmen found a cat in the cellar. The poor animal had been shut in there and forgotten. They should never have shown it to him."

"It was a lovely cat," said Simon, "even if it was dead. And it belonged to Amy Burgess. The men said so."

"It was wicked of them to tell that story to a small child." The rector seemed to have forgotten Emma. He spoke only to his son. "They just connected everything they could, Simon. Everything to do with death. That poor girl's murder was on everyone's mind – so they said it was her cat."

"It was," said Simon. "It still is."

The rector's head drooped, and Emma sensed that this was an old quarrel. They were dead-locked, and the silence between them grew until she could stand it no longer.

"The rain," she said, "it's getting worse. I'd better be getting home." It was a feeble excuse, but neither of them pressed her to stay.

The rain, however, did not turn out to be her friend. The rector's old car would not start. He couldn't call a patrolman because he had allowed his subscription to lapse, and the garage in the village was closed. There were, it seemed, no neighbours near enough to call on, and Emma's father could not pick her up because he was away from home all week with the car.

Simon was amused. "Well that's pretty comprehensive," he said. "You'll have to stay."

She wanted to object, but the rector said, "The one thing we don't lack in this house is space. Ring your mother and I'll have a word with her."

The rectory was even larger than she had imagined. Upstairs she and Simon passed several closed doors before they came to the spare room at the end of a corridor.

"You'll be quite comfortable," he said, "and you needn't worry about your mother. There's nobody like a parson for putting a mother's mind at rest."

"Where's your room?" she asked.

"Far away." He pointed to the other end of

the corridor beyond the head of the stairs. "For decency's sake."

She helped him make up the bed in her room. "This is a huge house for just two men," she said. "What's in all the other rooms?"

"Most of them are empty. My father sleeps downstairs next to his study so he can hear the phone. You and I are alone up here."

She busied herself smoothing the bedcover.

"Don't worry, Emma, I shan't come tapping at your door in the night." He loaned her his dressing gown. "Sorry I can't give you any pyjamas, I don't wear anything in bed."

"So that makes two of us tonight." She reddened. "I'll keep my door locked." But she did not draw back when he leant across the bed to kiss her.

They were still in each other's arms when the rain closed in and the evening darkened. "I like the rain," he murmured as she lay with her head on his shoulder. "We could be together out there."

"It's dark and cold."

"Dark and cold," he repeated, "where lovers meet. Should we go?"

"It's nicer here."

"No." He lifted his head, putting space between them. "They knew where to go, where to meet in the night."

"Who?" But she already knew.

"They went to the edge. They saw everything."

"It's lonely out there."

"Not lonely, Emma." She did not answer, and he said, "We would be with them."

To risk everything. To be where loving meant

dying. To surrender to the night. She trembled.

"You're not still afraid of me, are you?" he said softly.

"No. Of me." She pushed him gently away. "Leave me now."

"I can't. I won't."

"Please." It was too weak a word to undermine passion, and he clung fiercely to her until, forcing herself to reject him, she turned her head away.

Suddenly, he flung his arms wide and released her. "You mean it!" It was an accusation. In the grey light, as the rain stroked the window, his face had no expression. "You mean it." His voice had become dull. He went out and shut the door.

She lay where she was until all light had gone from the window and then she undressed and lay between the sheets. For a long time her eyes remained open but then, although she had not expected sleep to come to her, her eyelids closed and her breathing became as quiet as the empty spaces in the dark house.

She woke luxuriously in the darkness. It was the dead of night, but she was so warm she was sure she was not alone. No more than half awake, she clung to the dream that even as she slept she had been able to draw him to her. She stretched, sweeping her arms between the sheets to touch him. The bed was empty, but she knew he was near.

She listened. There was no sound. The rain had ceased after washing all night noises from the air, and the house held itself still, without a creak or a click in its ancient crevices. But she sensed that outside the door the silence had already shaped itself. He was standing there.

She slid out of bed, shivering for a moment as the night touched her skin, then put on his dressing gown, went softly across to the door and opened it slowly.

"Are you there?" Her whisper dissolved into the emptiness of the corridor. There was no answer. The night dimness of the room behind her merged into the shadows before her and she stood on the verge of nothingness.

"Is that you?" she said.

Something brushed the hem of her gown and she whisked it away, startled. The sudden movement made her stumble into the corridor, and once again something swished at the back of her legs and made her twist away. Her door, caught by the swirl of her gown, clicked shut. Reaching for it, she stumbled and fell.

She was on her knees in the darkness. The stairwell showed with a deeper blackness but beyond it, where the corridor ran to other bedrooms, she saw a thin vertical strip of yellow light. If Simon's door was open he must have left his room and be close to her.

"Where are you?" she whispered.

A faint sound answered her, as though his foot had brushed the wainscot.

"Don't do this." She raised her voice. "Say something!"

She was still crouching, about to stand up, when a faint scuffle near the floor made her lunge forward. Whatever it was that slid by her hand was not human. Her fingers, raking the air, came in contact with something brittle that, as soon as touched, retreated and she heard the scratch of small, hard feet.

Her breath sobbed in her throat and its echo frightened her. She clambered to her feet, clutching the gown close, and listened. She did not breathe. Whatever was there also held its breath.

"Simon!" Her strangled call was not loud enough, but now she was running towards the light. Something, ankle height, ran with her. She stopped. It ceased to move. She took a step. It stepped with her.

No going back. She dared not. Standing on tip-toe, her shoulders hunched and her arms pulled in, she breathed deeply, once, twice, then ran for the light. Claws rattled on floorboards alongside her, scurrying as fast as she ran, then faster until they were running ahead of her. But she did not slow. The light was her only hope.

She was still in the blackness of the corridor when whatever it was that ran with her reached the light. For a splinter of time she saw it. An animal, thin and familiar. She stopped and fought the pounding of her heart. A cat's outline. She was sure. Almost sure. Its shape was broken up by sparks of light from the tears in her eyes. But it was only a cat.

Emma moved forward and looked through the opening of the door.

Simon was in bed. He was awake, sitting up-right, and facing the door. As she watched, he smiled and put out a hand as if reaching for her.

She had begun to push the door wider when she saw that the smile was not meant for her.

His eyes were focused on the space between them where the cat was moving across the floor.

Emma felt herself begin to smile at her fears, but the smile did not materialize. There was something about the cat that was not right. It was ungainly, its movements were stiff, and as it leapt on to the bed she saw that it was very thin – so thin that its sides were hollow. And, when he lifted it and his hand began to stroke, she saw that it was worse than hollow.

She stood at the opening of the door and watched him caress the cat's sharp backbone. Its hair, uncared for, was spiky, and even his hands could not smooth it. And then, under his busy fingers, she saw that her eyes had not deceived her. There were points of light in its fur. The cat's flanks were pierced. Light showed through them. His fingers caressed the cavities. The rough fur was all that remained on the skeleton, and when the cat turned its head towards her she saw the sightless sockets of its dead head.

The night was silent, and remained so.

Nothing disturbed Emma as she dressed and stepped out into the dawn.

ORDINARY SEAMAN

John Gordon

Towards the end of the Second World War, the teenage John Gordon served as an Ordinary Seaman on board a minesweeper. He had some harrowing experiences; coming to terms with the peculiar traditions, practices and language of the Navy was a trial in itself... This fascinating memoir is his story.

MORE WALKER PAPERBACKS

For You to Enjoy